Hero

Anna Hackett

Hero

Published by Anna Hackett

Cover by Melody Simmons of eBookindiecovers
Edits by Tanya Saari

ISBN (eBook): 978-1-925539-09-7
ISBN (paperback): 978-1-925539-14-1

What readers are saying about Anna's Science Fiction Romance

Galactic Gladiators – Most Original Story Universe Winner 2016 – Gravetells

Gladiator – Two-time winner for Best Sci-fi Romance 2016 – Gravetells and Under the Covers

Hell Squad – Amazon Bestselling Science Fiction Romance Series and SFR Galaxy Award for best Post-Apocalypse for Readers who don't like Post-Apocalypse

At Star's End – One of Library Journal's Best E-Original Romances for 2014

Return to Dark Earth – One of Library Journal's Best E-Original Books for 2015 and two-time SFR Galaxy Awards winner

The Phoenix Adventures – SFR Galaxy Award Winner for Most Fun New Series and "Why Isn't This a Movie?" Series

Beneath a Trojan Moon – RWAus Ella Award Winner for Romantic Novella of the Year

"Like Indiana Jones meets Star Wars. A treasure hunt with a steamy romance." – SFF Dragon, review of *Among Galactic Ruins*

"Strap in, enjoy the heat of romance and the daring of this group of space travellers!" – Di, Top 500 Amazon Reviewer, review of *At Star's End*

"High action and adventure surrounding an impossible treasure hunt kept me reading until late in the night." – Jen, That's What I'm Talking About, review of *Beyond Galaxy's Edge*

"Action, danger, aliens, romance – yup, it's another great book from Anna Hackett!" – Book Gannet Reviews, review of *Hell Squad: Marcus*

Don't miss out! For updates about new releases, action romance info, free books, and other fun stuff, sign up for my VIP mailing list and get your *free box set* containing three action-packed romances.

Visit here to get started:
www.annahackettbooks.com

Chapter One

The sound echoed off the stone walls around him.

It wasn't thunder, or the roar of an engine. It was the combination of thousands of voices chanting his name.

Kace Tameron stood at the tunnel entrance and assimilated all the information. The heat of the setting suns on his skin. The thunder of the crowd sitting in the seats circling the arena. The bright strobe lights shining into the darkening sky.

His heartbeat stayed steady and he shifted his combat staff, the smooth steel cool and familiar against his palms. In his head, he ran through an Antarian fight chant to focus his thoughts.

Once he got the order, he'd step out onto the sand of the Kor Magna Arena.

It was the fiercest gladiatorial arena on the galaxy's outer rim. Where slaves fought for freedom, where fighters battled for glory, and where soldiers, like himself, came to hone their skills.

Around him, his fellow gladiators were stretching, checking their weapons, focusing their thoughts.

"I'm ready to smack some Thraxians into the sand," Thorin shouted, slapping the head of his axe against his palm.

Kace eyed the giant Sirrush gladiator. Thorin was a little wild and deadly on the sand. His fighting partner stood beside him, the champion of the Kor Magna Arena, Raiden Tiago. The man's tattoos gleamed on his bronze skin, and there was no missing the fact that he was built like a fighter, and not the prince he'd once been.

Just beyond them in the tunnel stood another fighting pair from the House of Galen. Mountainous Nero and showman Lore. Kace was a career soldier. He'd worked with some of the best fighters on his planet, but this team was beyond good.

Here, projectile weapons were banned and considered dishonorable. Here, most technology was frowned upon, too. Here, you fought up close and personal, and you had to be good.

It was one of the cardinal rules of the arena—and there weren't many rules in Kor Magna—that a gladiator not be enhanced, or controlled by tech. They fought robots, used some energy shields and weapons, and raced chariots. But at the end of the day, it was gladiator against gladiator, man against man.

Someone bumped his shoulder, and Kace looked down at his own fighting partner. Saff Essikani was grinning at him, her teeth white against her darker skin. Her long, black hair fell to her waist in a mass of tiny braids. She was tall and muscular, and a hell of a gladiator in the arena.

While eagerness wafted off Saff, Kace stayed still and composed.

He wasn't an arena slave fighting for freedom, or a lifer like his friends, who considered the desert world of Carthago and the city of Kor Magna home. Kace was military. Born and bred to fight. He was here on a contract for two years to hone his skills.

A man stepped in front of them, wearing all black. His black shirt covered one arm and left his other muscled bicep bare. He moved his powerful body with a precision that let you know he could burst into action when required. Kace recognized a fellow warrior when he saw one.

With a scarred face and a black eye patch over one eye, Galen, Imperator of the House of Galen, was an imposing man.

"I don't need to tell any of you to fight well. You do every time you step in the arena." His single icy-blue eye took them all in. "I will tell you that the House of Thrax is still very unhappy with us."

Kace knew that was an understatement. They'd rescued several women from the Thraxians, and beaten the aliens time and again. Kace felt a very un-soldier-like lick of satisfaction. The Thraxians were slavers, and they deserved everything they got. They snatched people from all over the galaxy to sell to the highest bidders, and they'd made the unfortunate mistake of taking a transient wormhole to a distant star system on the opposite side of the galaxy.

They'd abducted a group of women off a space

station near a planet called Earth. The diminutive women had also proven to be very tough and fierce. Thinking of them almost made him smile. The Thraxians hadn't known what hit them.

Kace, along with the other gladiators in the House of Galen, had helped free the Earth women. And now Harper, Regan, and Rory were stranded here, unable to return to their planet.

"The House of Thrax is looking for revenge," Galen said, his voice deep. "Watch yourselves out there."

Kace tightened his grip on his staff. It was of typical Antarian design—his people made some of the best weapons in the known galaxy. In the military, he also used ranged weapons, but here in the arena, it was considered cowardly. His proficiency with the staff had increased substantially in the six months he'd been a member of the House of Galen.

Right now, he was ready to pit himself against the Thraxian gladiators.

He heard footsteps behind them. He turned his head and he saw Harper, one of the women of Earth, move forward. Her smile was centered on Raiden.

"We came to wish you luck," Harper said.

The tough gladiator snatched the woman up with one arm, and pulled her in for a kiss. She was far shorter than her lover, but Kace had fought with her in the arena, and she was a hell of a fighter. Watching the two of them together made something in Kace's chest tighten.

Love was a foreign concept on Antar. In fact, it was expressly forbidden. It was fascinating to see the emotion shining off this couple.

Another woman moved forward. Dr. Regan Forrest was even shorter than Harper. Her flowing white dress accented her full curves and billowed out as she threw herself into Thorin's brawny arms.

Kace resisted shaking his head. Of all the gladiators in the House of Galen, he would never have picked big, wild Thorin to fall for a tiny, sweet Earth girl.

Unwillingly, Kace's gaze searched for the final woman from Earth.

There she was. Aurora Fraser, better known as Rory.

She was short as well, but somewhere between Regan and Harper in height. She didn't have Regan's curves, or Harper's athletic physique. She was built straight up and down, with slim hips, and toned arms. She wasn't wearing a dress like Regan, or fighting leathers like Harper. Instead, she wore simple black trousers and a white shirt that wrapped around her body, hugging small, high breasts. Her unique red hair fell in a wild tangle of curls around her face. Green-gold eyes watched everyone and everything, and a faint smile flirted on her lips.

She'd suffered horribly at the hands of the Thraxians. Then, they'd sold her to the deplorable Vorn. She'd been beaten, treated worse than an animal, but here she was, smiling.

The women of Earth were tough, stubborn, and strong.

Her green-gold gaze met his and she moved closer. "Ready to fight, pretty boy?"

"Always." He fought the urge to tell her not to use that silly name. He was an Antarian soldier, there was nothing pretty about him. She'd called him that from the moment he'd rescued her in the House of Vorn. She'd also given him a black eye during the rescue.

If there was one thing Kace had already learned about Rory Fraser, it was that she swung her fists first and asked questions later.

She boldly eyed him up and down. "I believe it. I'm excited to see you fight."

Kace paused for a second, absorbing the fact that she was going to be watching him tonight. Something inside him liked that.

"Do you get nervous?" she asked.

"No."

He saw her nose wrinkle, and that drew his attention to the interesting splash of dots across the bridge of it. Freckles, she called them.

"Not at all?"

"No." Antarian soldiers didn't feel nerves.

She rolled her eyes. "Okay, gladiator. Well, be careful out there."

"All right, time to move," Galen called out.

Kace gave Rory a nod, even as he noted Raiden planting a huge kiss on Harper. Kace wondered for a brief second what Rory's lips felt like.

Then he shook his head and turned. Sex wasn't

outlawed on Antar, nor was it endorsed. Soldiers were encouraged to pour all their emotions into their training, not frivolous activities.

He walked out of the tunnel, lifting his staff and centering his thoughts.

Together, the House of Galen gladiators stepped out onto the sand.

Around them, rows and rows of arena seats were packed full of people. When the crowd saw them, they roared their approval.

Thorin shook his axe in the air, while Saff pumped her fists at the crowd. Lore did a turn and tossed something in the air. Fireworks flew upward and broke off in all directions in silver and red—the House of Galen colors. Nero scowled at him.

Raiden barely paid the crowd any attention, his red cloak flaring behind him as he strode into the heart of the arena. He'd never pandered to the spectators, and he'd still become champion. He was a warrior at heart, and Kace followed his example.

As the others called out to the crowd, Kace knelt and picked up a handful of sand. He let it run through his fingers. He never let himself forget that here, he would be tested and challenged. These weren't fights to the death, but injuries always happened. Blood would splatter the sand. He wasn't here for the glory, he was here for duty and honor.

The tenor of the crowd changed, and Kace straightened.

Their opponents had entered the arena.

He moved to join his team, and saw the

Thraxian gladiators coming toward them. Not all the warriors in the House of Thrax were Thraxians, but tonight, most of them were.

They made an impact. Seven feet tall, with powerful muscled bodies, the Thraxians had tough, brown skin, and a set of black horns on their heads. Their eyes glowed orange, and it matched the glow of orange veins visible through their skin.

Saff stepped up beside him. "Ready, military man?"

"Ready."

As the Thraxian gladiators moved into a jog, loping toward them, Raiden turned, a hard look on his face. "For honor and freedom."

"For honor and freedom." Kace raised his voice to join the others. They broke into a run and raced to meet the enemy.

Kace swung his staff, cracking it against the sword of a Thraxian fighter. He spun, bending one knee, and moving his staff upward. It was a fast move, and the Thraxian barely had time to react. The weapon slammed into the alien's side. With a roar, he staggered backward.

Again, Kace swung his staff, and again. His weapon was like an extension of himself. Soon, the Thraxian fell to his knees in the sand, and Kace brought the staff down on the back of the man's neck.

Thwack. The Thraxian plummeted to the sand. Kace leaped over the top of the fallen man and kept moving. He flanked Saff, and they both stared up at the giant Thraxian charging at them. He towered over both of them.

The female gladiator lifted a small, egg-shaped device. Kace nodded and watched as she tossed it at the giant.

The device exploded outward, and a wire-mesh net flew at their opponent. It tangled around his lower half, tripping him over. As he struggled, Kace leaped up, his staff raised above his head. He swung it down and slammed it against the man's lower back. He heard the crack of bones, and the Thraxian roared.

"Nice work." Saff slapped Kace's arm.

They continued to fight through the crowd of gladiators. Nero and Lore fought with determination and a lethal grace. Thorin and Raiden plowed through their opponents.

Finally, Kace pulled to a stop, as Thorin and Raiden engaged the last of the Thraxians. Kace rested the end of his staff in the sand and looked toward the stands.

His gaze zeroed in on the House of Galen seats, down close to the arena floor. Instantly, he spotted that brilliant glow of red hair. He saw that Rory was watching him, grinning.

"Incoming," Saff called out.

Kace whipped his head back and saw a gladiator had broken free from Thorin and Raiden. He was racing toward Saff and Kace. This one was a Gavia. A reptilian species that could spit poison.

Saff tossed her net device up and down in her palm, watching and waiting. When she got like this, she reminded Kace of a hunting cat, patient and cunning.

Usually, Saff was all fire and unrelenting power when she fought. Patience was Kace's skill, not Saff's. More often than not, she charged in without planning.

But this time, Kace didn't want to wait. He felt an extra rush of energy this evening, a need to show off his skills. He rushed forward to meet the gladiator.

Kace used his most dramatic moves, swinging his staff in a wild, lethal dance. He wore the other man down, slamming the staff into him at all the sensitive spots on the Gavia's body. The alien groaned, swinging wildly and spitting green blood onto the sand. His movements were slowing, losing coordination.

Then Kace swung the staff sideways, taking the Gavia down at the knees. He swung again and caught the alien under his jaw, slamming his head back. As the Gavia cursed, he moved his head, and a shower of dark-green poison sprayed out of the alien's mouth.

Kace dived, rolled through the sand, and came back up on his feet. He could hear the poison sizzling on the sand. Again, he swung his staff around and caught the Gavia in the back. The alien fell forward on his hands and knees, struggling to get back up. Then, finally, he collapsed.

The crowd went wild.

Saff appeared beside him, one dark brow arched. "Well, look who ate his Wheaties today."

Kace frowned. *Wheaties*? "I don't know what you're talking about."

"It's a phrase that Regan taught me. Means you ate something that gave you some extra energy today."

Kace didn't respond. Another House of Thrax gladiator was back up, and lumbering toward them. He was big, muscles bulging across his broad chest and wide shoulders. His name was Naare, a Varinid from the planet Varin. He'd been a gladiator with the House of Thrax for years. Kace kind of liked the guy, and knew he had almost earned his freedom. He was very good with an axe.

Naare engaged, swinging his weapon in a wild arc. Saff and Kace ducked and rolled.

Kace spun, bringing his staff up. He struck Naare in the side, then the shoulder.

Kace frowned. The Varinid was usually lightning-fast on his feet. Today, he was slower than a green recruit. Again and again, Kace swung his staff into his opponent, while the other man never got a hit near him.

Naare's eyes were dull. Another two hits of the staff, and the gladiator went down.

Kace frowned. Naare was close to gaining his freedom, and he usually was a challenging opponent.

But tonight, something was different. Maybe Naare had picked up a drug habit? Kor Magna drew spectators from around the galaxy for the fights, but outside the arena walls, the city—and its shiny, glitzy District—catered to a lot of vices.

Gambling, drugs, women, men...whatever you wanted, you could find it here. Kace was well aware more than one gladiator in the arena dealt with their demons through the use of chemicals.

Suddenly, the wail of a siren echoed out over the arena. He heard the announcers calling out, declaring the House of Galen the winners.

Kace wiped his arm across his face, brushing away the blood and sweat. Right here, right now in this moment, he felt a clarity he rarely felt anywhere else.

On Antar, with his squad of soldiers, he'd always felt part of a team, fighting to protect their planet.

But it wasn't until he'd come to the arena that he'd truly felt alive. Here in the arena, he'd learned a lot—about fighting, about strategy, about people. What he hadn't expected was to make friends.

A big fist punched into his shoulder. "Hey there, military man." Thorin hit him again. "What got into you tonight?"

Raiden slid his sword back into his scabbard. "You used some pretty fancy moves out there."

Kace shrugged. "I was in the mood."

"You were just showing off," Saff teased.

"An Antarian soldier does not show off."

His friends continued to rib him as they crossed the sand. As they neared the tunnel, he looked up at the House of Galen seats. He saw Rory at the railing watching him. She was jumping up and down, her arms above her head. He watched as she put her fingers to her mouth and let out a shrill whistle.

Kace's gut hardened as realization set in. *Drak*. It hadn't just been a need to test his skills. The reason he'd acted out of character was sitting in the stands, celebrating his win.

Chapter Two

Rory sat on the bed, surrounded by a scatter of electronics parts.

There were wires, randomly shaped pieces of metal, and a bunch of things she didn't even recognize. She picked up a small, gel-filled pouch, frowning at it. As far as she could tell, it was some sort of biological component, and it was fascinating. Since her rescue, she'd been spending a lot of her time trying to figure out how technology here on Carthago worked.

Once an engineer, always an engineer.

Even when that engineer had been abducted by aliens, and was currently living with a bunch of galactic gladiators. With a sigh, she picked up the neat little engineering tool that Regan had gotten for her. The rest of the stuff Rory had either scavenged from the trash, begged the House of Galen maintenance team for, or asked Galen to source for her.

Galen. Now, there was one scary dude. One icy look from Galen was enough to have you shaking in your—she glanced at her feet—sandals. Still, however badass the imperator was, he'd taken her in, taken them all in, and for that, she was grateful.

He'd given her a room, clothes, and food. She rubbed a hand over her hip and the top of her buttock, feeling a slight lump. She'd even been given a thorough medical check, including a contraceptive health implant, by Galen's fancy team of healers.

Rory touched her tool to one of the wires and saw a faint spark. She was damn happy to find that a lot of the technology here was actually lower-tech than on Earth. Sure, it was still different, but most of it wasn't too difficult to work out. Some of it, on the other hand...she held up something that looked like a spiral made from a glowing blue rock. It pulsed gently in her palm. Well, some of it was going to take some time for her to decipher.

A warm breeze flowed in through the open window, ruffling the sheer curtains. She should be asleep, like everyone else in the House of Galen at this time of night. But as usual, Rory couldn't.

She tossed the tool down. She'd enjoyed the fight this evening, the energy and excitement of it. It had been brutal, but Rory was trained in mixed martial arts, and she'd seen loads of fights. In fact, she'd even participated in a few of her own.

But even after the excitement of the night had worn off, even after a few drinks with the celebrating gladiators, and though she felt weary, she just couldn't sleep. Most nights since she'd been rescued, ugly, ugly nightmares of her captivity still liked to pay her a visit.

Damned uninvited guests.

With a disgusted sigh, she tossed the tool and the electronic part on the bed. She stared at the soft blue cover, and then around the nice room. Moonlight was shining in through the large, arched window. She pushed off the bed and walked over to the window.

The moon looked huge in the sky, and far bigger and brighter than Earth's moon. A pang of longing and loneliness hit her. She missed her family desperately. Her mother's firm hugs, her dad's quiet comments, and her brothers' incessant teasing and commentary on her life.

She missed her favorite Indonesian-brewed beer. She missed her favorite sushi restaurant. God, and she missed her well-stocked toolbox, filled with all her carefully selected and carefully maintained tools. It had been in her locker back on Fortuna Space Station…so it was probably now just space junk orbiting Jupiter.

Rory pressed the heels of her hands to her eyes, like she could push back the tears. She wasn't a crier. She detested crying. But it was pretty darn hard *not to*, when you learned that your planet was on the other side of the galaxy and you had no way home.

She pressed a hand to the window arch, the stone warm under her hand. She knew she had a lot to be thankful for. Regan and Harper were with her, and they were safe here in the House of Galen. Just the thought of the Thraxians and the Vorn had memories hitting her like hard blows. The cells, the depravity, the beatings, the hunger, the cold, the pain.

And Madeline Cochran, the civilian commander of Fortuna Space Station, was still out there. Still trapped and somebody's prisoner.

Shit. No sleep for Rory.

Rory strode back to the bed and grabbed the small makeshift toolbox she'd been putting together for herself. She'd found the small, metallic box in a storage room, and it was just the right size for her to lug around.

She headed out of her room. If she couldn't sleep, she'd damn well find something to fix.

Since she'd dismantled her mom's computer at the age of seven, Rory had loved building and fixing things. She loved knowing how things worked, and how they fit together. It always, without fail, calmed the noise in her head.

She remembered being an energetic child, and then a pretty high-maintenance teenager. She'd always been filled with energy, and a little high-strung. Her mom and dad had constantly shoved things at her to fix to keep her busy.

When Rory had been in the gym earlier with Harper, a space just off the smaller training arena, she'd noticed one of the wall lights wasn't working. She was going to make herself useful in her new home.

She headed through the tunnels and down one level to the gym area. It was filled with sand-colored mats, and bags hanging from the roof. There was a roped-off, indoor fighting ring in the back corner.

Thankfully, there were no treadmills or other torturous exercise equipment. Rory hated sweating her butt off and going nowhere.

She reached the doorway, and heard a noise from inside. Rhythmic puffs of breath.

She paused in the doorway. Kace was doing push-ups on the mats.

A warm tingle ran through her belly. Here was another thing to be grateful for—first-class gladiator eye-candy. The clean-cut gladiator was wearing soft, dark trousers, and no shirt. All that glorious bronze skin...she leaned against the doorway and couldn't drag her gaze off him.

He was all sharply defined muscles, and she could see each one flex in his strong back as he moved. Under the soft fabric of his trousers, she saw the impressive curve of his ass and the strong muscles of his thighs.

He just kept moving up and down, like a well-maintained machine. Focused. Driven.

She'd wondered more than once if Kace ever relaxed. Whenever she was around him, he had this coiled strength, an intense tension, that warned her he could explode into action in a millisecond.

She stepped inside. "Hey, pretty boy. Don't you ever run out of steam?"

Kace paused and turned his head. His brown hair was slightly damp against his well-shaped head. He pushed to his feet. "Steam? I have no steam."

Rory shook her head. The translator device the Thraxians had implanted at the base of her neck meant she could understand other people's languages and they could understand her. But her Earth sayings tended to catch people off guard. "Energy. Don't you ever run out of energy?"

"No. A soldier knows how to manage his energy levels."

He was handsome any way you looked at him. He made her think of an action hero. Strong jaw, the sharp blades of his cheekbones, and brilliant blue eyes.

Rory shifted. He was so damn delicious, and so not her type. She'd always liked bad boys and rebels. Musicians, artists…hell, she'd even dated a biker once.

Kace was a big, bad gladiator, but he was also as clean-cut and controlled as they came.

"The fight was great," she said. "You were wicked with the staff. Congrats on your win."

He inclined his head. "It is very late. You should be sleeping."

She fiddled with the handle of her toolbox. "I…couldn't. Thought I'd do something productive instead." She gestured to the toolbox.

"You have trouble sleeping?"

Great. Her insomnia and nightmares were the last thing she wanted to discuss. "I keep thinking about poor Madeline."

Rory knew Kace and the others were helping to search for Madeline. To the galaxy, the gladiators of the House of Galen were simply fighters on the bloody sand of the arena. Behind the scenes, they were heroes. They rescued imprisoned, stolen and injured gladiator recruits from the other houses. From scum like the Thraxians.

Rory would never forget that they'd rescued her and her friends.

"Have you heard anything about Madeline?" she asked.

His blue eyes flashed. "No. I'm sorry."

Rory's shoulders sagged.

"Galen is doing everything he can to find her."

Rory nodded and moved over to the bank of lights on the wall. She knelt between one that was completely out, and another neighboring one that was flickering beside it. She opened her toolbox, grabbed what passed for a screwdriver on Carthago, and started prying the cover off the malfunctioning light.

"Madeline was your friend?"

Rory glanced over her shoulder. "Not really. She was in charge of the space station where we worked. Madeline can be...well, a real bitch. She kept herself apart from the space station employees and didn't seem to have any friends. But none of that matters. She's human, and no one deserves captivity with the Thraxians." A shiver ran through Rory.

"We'll find her."

Kace moved closer and Rory could smell him. *Mm-mmm.* Healthy male sweat. She made what she hoped to be a sound of acknowledgment in her throat.

"Galen has a vast network of contacts. Someone will know something."

Rory suddenly realized she was staring at the wall, sniffing Kace's scent. She cleared her throat and stuck her tool inside the inner workings of the light. She knew because of the unique power system there was no risk of her being zapped. She'd been shadowing a few of the maintenance team workers when she got the chance, and peppering them with questions. She didn't recognize anything familiar inside the light, so she started tapping around inside, trying to work it out.

She could feel Kace's attention on her, and then sensed when he crouched down close by. His big body brushed against hers in a featherlight touch.

"You've been fixing lots of things around here."

She paused. *He'd been watching her?*

"You don't have to," he continued.

"I know, but I like it. I'm learning lots about the different technology from the maintenance team. Besides, Harper fights in the arena, and Regan fiddles in her lab and invents fabulous new substances that Galen can sell. I fix things. It's the least I can do. It's how I can contribute."

"You have a safe place here." Kace rested his hand on her shoulder.

That simple touch burned through her. She'd spent a long time locked in a cell by the Thraxians and knew she was touch-deprived. She felt the warmth of him radiating against her skin. Rory found she desperately wanted to know more about him.

"Thanks. I know. But I'm not the type to sit about doing nothing. I do have some fight training, so I may try the arena." Her brothers had started martial-arts training in their teens. At first, they'd been horrified when their baby sister had wanted to follow in their footsteps. After some spectacular nagging, her parents had let her. Rory was stubborn when she wanted something, and refused to give in. "Harper is teaching me to use the sword, and Saff promised to help me learn the net." Rory tilted her head. "They say you're the best with the staff. Would you show me some moves?"

This close to him, she saw the scowl that crossed his face. His fingers tightened on her shoulder.

"You will not fight in the arena."

She blinked. "Well, maybe not right now, but who knows, one day I might give it a try."

"No."

Her gaze narrowed. "At what point did I give you the impression that I would take orders from you, pretty boy?"

"You are too small and delicate for the arena."

Rory stared at him, gobsmacked, then threw her head back and laughed. "I've never been called small or delicate in my life."

His gaze ran over her face, like she was some sort of puzzle for him to decode.

"Look, for now I just want to learn the different weapons," she told him. "I've been warned that Kor Magna isn't the safest city in the galaxy. I thought it would be a good idea to know the best ways to defend myself."

His fingers flexed on her shoulder. "Of course. I would be happy to show you some moves with the staff." He stood abruptly. "I have to go. Good night, Rory."

What bug had gotten up his butt? She watched him disappear. It was like he wore an icy, controlled shell. One that showed no signs of cracking.

With a sigh, Rory turned back to the lights and resumed tapping the components. She was going to fix something, dammit.

***

Kace stepped out of the arena tunnels and into the bright morning sunshine. He paused, looking around, as Galen and Raiden stepped out beside him, followed by Rory.

Kace automatically moved so he was close to her and able to subtly maneuver her into the center of their small group.

She looked tired, dark circles under her eyes, but she was still looking around the city street with interest.

They were going to the Kor Magna District.

Kace hated the District. There was too much of everything. Too much noise, too much flash, too many people. Too many vices and too much weakness. He could see the tops of the tall, glass-covered buildings ahead, spearing sharply into the pale blue sky. Even in the bright sunshine, lights were blinking, huge screens advertising the latest shows, fights, and games. He knew the casinos would be packed with aliens from all over the galaxy, betting their last credits at the tables.

"Let's get to Zhim's place," Galen said.

They crossed a cobblestone-paved road. They were going to see Kor Magna's most prominent information merchant. Kace disliked Zhim almost as much as the District.

"Zhim's the best person to find information on Madeline," Galen said. "He specifically requested to talk to you, Rory. To find out what you might know that could help him track down your friend."

Rory nodded. She was wearing a pair of tight black trousers and a top in a green that matched the green in her eyes. Kace wondered if she'd slept last night. He remembered the way she'd looked in the gym, the way she'd laughed with such abandon. Even late in the night, and tired, Rory burned with a bright light.

"Don't give Zhim any extra information," Raiden warned. "Information is his drug. The man will do whatever he can to try and squeeze it out of you."

"And then he'll buy and sell it. He'd buy or sell anything," Kace added darkly.

Rory nodded again. "Sounds like a real winner. Okay boys, lead the way."

They walked down a narrow backstreet, which slowly gave way to the wider avenue that ran through the heart of the District. The low, older buildings of the main part of the city slowly gave way to the slick, shiny casinos.

There was nothing like the District on Antar.

Kace's people admired restraint and order. In Antar's cities, practical, well-built and defensible buildings were interspersed with elegant parks. In the District, it was all pavement and glass and lights.

He watched as Rory slowed down, trying to peer inside the shiny glass doors of a casino they were passing. People of all species were flowing in and out. He gently nudged her back to keep her moving.

They passed a giant fountain that shot jets of water into the air in a beautiful, hypnotic dance. Lights changed the color of the water in time to music that was playing. Rory peered into the water, and when she spotted the various water creatures frolicking in the crystal-blue pool, she gasped.

"Zhim lives in the tallest apartment building in the District." Galen nodded to the glass spire ahead. "In the penthouse."

The building was made of smoky, dark glass with a wide base that narrowed at the top to a point.

They entered the building, and after a quick talk with security, they entered a glass bubble set in the wall.

"Wow. Cool elevator." Rory was studying the neon glow of the controls that appeared on the glass.

Galen touched the controls and they shot smoothly upward. Light flooded the small space. The bubble moved up the outside of the building, offering a stunning view of the District below. Rory gasped, and without fear, stepped close to the glass. She laughed with obvious glee.

It reminded Kace that she'd been kept in a cell for a very long time. Anger was a shot to his system. He hated any being who hurt those who weren't as strong as themselves.

The speed of the elevator and the dizzying view didn't bother Kace, but he tugged Rory back. He didn't want her too close to that glass wall.

Finally, the elevator slowed and the doors opened. They stepped out onto a wide terrace. A breeze blew at them, ruffling Rory's red curls.

"Now, this is a view worth paying for." She moved toward the railing. Kace had to admit that Zhim had a hell of a view to wake up to.

Up this high, you could see beyond the far edges of the city, and into the desert stretching off into the distance. The dull, beige-colored sand dominated, but in the distance he could make out a patch of large sand dunes and a white area that he knew must be some sort of dried-out lake. Off to the left, just a dark smudge on the horizon, were the Crixis Mountains—a strange mix of flat-topped mesas and ragged spikes of rock.

"Welcome to my domain," a deep male voice said.

Chapter Three

The information merchant strode toward them. He was tall with a firm body, although he carried far less bulk than the gladiators. A wide smile topped a face full of sharp angles and eyes that tilted up at the sides.

Zhim wore a flowing white shirt and elegant trousers that Kace wouldn't be caught dead in. His feet were bare.

"So…" Zhim came forward, his strange multi-colored eyes zeroed in on Rory. "You are Aurora Shannon Fraser of Earth."

He reached out, as though he was going to touch her.

Kace reached out and caught the man's wrist. Zhim stilled, then turned his palm over and grinned. As if Kace had told him an interesting story.

"Call me Aurora again, and I'll hit you," Rory said in a friendly tone lined with very sharp teeth.

Raiden snorted, and Kace had to struggle to hide his own smile.

"Beautiful with an edge." Zhim tilted his head, a strand of his long, dark hair escaping the tie at the back of his neck. "Fascinating."

"I'm not here to fascinate you, Mr. Zhim. I'm here to ask about my friend."

"Come, come." He waved them over to some couches that were set out on the terrace. A beautiful woman with long, platinum-colored hair and wearing a flowing pink dress came out of the large open doors, carrying a tray of drinks. She set the tray down on the table and hurried away without a word.

Zhim settled on a couch, sprawling back against the cushions like a king in his palace. "So, you are searching for Madeline Renee Cochran. Commander of the Fortuna Space Station."

As always, Kace wondered where the hell Zhim got his information from.

Rory perched on the edge of a couch. "Yes. Have you heard anything?"

Zhim shrugged and picked up a small, jewel-colored glass. He waved at the tray. "Please, help yourselves. It's made from the juice of the *tuava* fruit. Expensive and tasty."

The gladiators didn't move, but Kace watched Rory shrug. She took one of the drinks, sniffed it, then took a sip.

"It pains me to tell you this..." an unhappy scowl crossed the man's face. "But I have no information on the location of Ms. Cochran."

Rory's shoulders slumped. Kace moved closer, quelling the urge to touch her.

"So why are we here?" Rory set her glass down. "I've been told you are the king of information. That you're a master of finding it and selling it."

She sniffed. "I guess that was all an exaggeration."

Zhim straightened, and Kace stifled another smile. The information merchant's eyes narrowed. He clearly didn't like not having the information.

"Rory," Zhim drawled. "If the information was available, I would have it."

She leaned forward. "Madeline is here on Carthago, somewhere. I saw her in the cell beside mine at the House of Thrax. Someone knows where she is. They clearly have the information, and you don't."

Zhim's mouth opened, then closed.

Rory tucked a red curl behind her ear. "I think this is a waste of time. I think we'll have better luck if Galen just asks around. Or if Raiden, Kace, and the others search the city—"

"I will find her," Zhim bit out.

Rory lifted her hand, looking at her nails. "I'll believe it when I see it."

Kace couldn't control his smile anymore. He glanced at Raiden and Galen. Raiden had a huge smile on his face, and even Galen's lips had tilted up.

"Feisty." Zhim tossed back his drink and set the glass down. "I like that."

Kace felt his jaw tense. A gleam had come into Zhim's multi-colored eyes. He stared at Rory like she was a sweet, expensive treat. Kace's hand curled into a fist.

"You'll tap your extended networks?" Galen asked.

"It'll cost you."

"It always does," Galen said dryly.

Zhim glanced back at Rory. "I may give you a discount for bringing me a pretty girl to chat with."

Kace leaned forward, but Rory slapped a hand against his chest. She shot Zhim a sugary smile. "And I might punch you in the nose."

The blue-green colors in Zhim's eyes swirled, and Kace shook his head. The guy was enjoying this.

Rory stood. "Well, Zhim, it's been…interesting."

"I wholeheartedly agree." The information merchant stood, the breeze making his shirt flutter. "I do hope you come back and visit me again…Aurora."

Rory moved fast, slamming her fist into Zhim's gut. He doubled over and grunted.

"I warned you," she said.

Zhim grinned. "It was worth it."

Rory shook her head. As they moved back to the elevator, Kace could hear Zhim laughing. The elevator doors closed, and the bubble started downward.

"I hate him," Kace muttered.

"He annoys everybody," Galen said.

"I didn't mind him," Rory said.

Kace stared at her. "You *liked* him?"

She shrugged. "He's annoying, but I can tell he's smart, if a little crazy. I don't mind a little crazy."

Kace knew no one would ever describe him as crazy. He frowned at her. "That's the kind of man you like?"

Her eyes met his, held for a second. "I don't have

a type, pretty boy." She crossed her arms over her chest and let her gaze drift down his body. "I'm an equal-opportunity kind of girl."

Kace blinked and heard Raiden chuckle.

Rory turned to Galen. "You're sure he'll find the information to track down Madeline?"

"He's our best bet," the imperator replied.

The elevator slowed and the doors opened.

"Okay, let's get back to the House of Galen." Galen's ice-blue eye glittered. "I have some other people I can contact as well, but I'm running out of options. Whatever the Thraxians have done with Madeline, they've hidden her deep."

Despair flashed across Rory's face before she pulled herself together.

Raiden and Galen pushed open the doors and stepped outside. Kace followed with Rory. Out of habit, he scanned the street. There were too many people, and too many transports. Feeling suddenly uneasy, he stayed closer to Rory.

Suddenly, she stopped and grabbed his arm.

"I really don't have a type, but I do have to tell you that all of a sudden, big, tough and slightly uptight gladiator is working for me."

He felt like he'd taken a fist to his chest.

"Rory—"

She leaned closer and, at that second, a projectile whizzed past her head. It hit the window behind them, shattering the glass.

Kace moved, tackling her. They rolled across the pavement.

More shots peppered the ground around them. *Drak*!

Kace yanked Rory into his arms, lifted her off her feet, and leaped up. He ran, pushing for all the speed he could.

More projectiles fired, and more glass shattered around them. Rory buried her head against his chest. He felt a hard punch to his side, and his body jerked. *Drak*, he was hit. Ignoring the wound, he kept running.

He heard people screaming, and the whine of transport engines.

"Kace!" Raiden's shout.

Raiden and Galen flanked them. Galen had an energy shield up, generated from a metallic band on his wrist. He stepped in front of them. More shots hit, disintegrating as they struck the large, blue barrier.

"Get into the closest casino," Galen called out.

They all shuffled backward, up some steps, and into the casino's front door. Inside was a hubbub of people holding frothing drinks and huddled around tables playing cards and holo games.

Kace set Rory down. "Are you okay? Were you hit?"

She shook her head, scraping her hair back. "I'm fine. But oh, my God, you're bleeding. Were you *shot*?"

He felt the warm slide of blood at his lower back, soaking into his trousers. "It'll keep. First, we need to get you to safety." They needed to get back to the House of Galen. Fast.

"It'll keep?" her voice rose. "What do you mean, *it'll keep*? You've been shot." She moved to lift up his shirt.

He grabbed her hands. "Rory. I'm Antarian, we have a high tolerance to pain and can manipulate our bodies. I've slowed blood flow to the wound and dampened the pain."

Her brows rose. "You can do that?"

He nodded and turned her. "Come on. We need to go." Kace could see Galen and Raiden were already assessing the best way out. They'd attracted some attention, but most of the people in the room looked bleary-eyed and far more interested in playing their games.

"God, it looks like someone vomited a rainbow over the place." Rory shuddered.

The casino was very colorful. He saw walls painted different shimmering hues and the ceiling was a swirl of colors. Tall, slender servers walked through the crowd, balancing large trays of drinks and wearing uniforms in virulent pink, blue, and yellow.

"This way," Galen said with a nod of his head.

Kace scooped up Rory again and moved through the crowd.

"Kace, I can walk! You're hurt."

"Shh." He tightened his arms around her. No one was getting to her again.

"You're so damn stubborn." She shifted in his arms, and tore a strip of fabric off the bottom of her shirt. Then she reached around him and pressed it against the bleeding wound on his back. "I don't care if you can slow the bleeding and stop it hurting. You want to bleed to death just to prove how tough you are. Typical man."

She gently touched his injury, and Kace battled a flood of conflicting emotions. No one had ever cared for him when he was injured. Sure, they dumped him in a regen tank in Medical, but he was a fierce Antarian soldier. From birth, Antarian children weren't coddled—no hugs, no one to fuss over scraped knees, no one to help ease the pain.

"There is no need—"

"Shut up," she snapped.

Bemused, Kace did that and focused on getting her out of there. As they passed through the crowd, he watched Rory taking it all in. The packed tables with holo games projected into the air, the machines with blinking lights and grating music with players lined up three deep to have a turn.

"Well, these aren't blackjack tables and poker machines," Rory said, "but this place looks pretty darn similar to casinos on Earth."

They passed a Robinid alien being carried on a golden litter by four giant humanoids. Rory's mouth dropped open. The Robinid had deep blue skin, an overlarge head, and several tentacles.

"Okay, not quite like Earth," she murmured.

They skirted around a dance floor and a crowd of people were dancing and jumping to the deafening music. Dancers were grinding against each other, some kissing and fondling each other in plain sight.

That was the District. Whatever you wanted, whenever you wanted, and right where you were standing.

Soon, they were moving out of the main casino area and into a corridor. Galen waved them through a door and into the kitchens.

"Holy cow," Rory breathed.

Several workers and chefs bustled around the long benches and steam rose off the cook tops. A chef stirred a large pan and blue flames shot into the air. But Rory was staring at the huge tank set along one wall. Inside, all manner of aquatic creatures swam idly. Some larger than Rory herself.

"The clientele pay very well to have the freshest of everything," he said.

They reached a back entrance and stepped out into a narrow alley. Galen and Raiden were tense and alert.

Kace arched his head, looking at the rooftops. "I don't like this." Too many places for a sniper.

"I don't either," Galen said with a frown. "Let's make it quick."

Here, the District wasn't so pretty. There were several overflowing industrial trash receptacles and a rotten, damp stench that seared Kace's nostrils. They hurried through the alley. He wouldn't be happy until they were back inside the arena walls.

Suddenly, projectiles slammed into the wall behind them. Kace bent his body over Rory's, hearing her cry. He raced for cover, seeing Galen and Raiden running in front of them.

Green laser fire lit up the alley and guards dressed in black uniforms surrounded them. The stone-faced men and women fired their laser pistols up toward the sniper's location on the roof.

What the drak? Kace straightened, looking at their unknown saviors.

"Sir, the gunman is gone," a female guard said, looking beyond Kace's shoulder.

Kace turned. A man dressed in a black suit and a crisp white shirt was striding toward them, black hair brushing his shoulders. With a loose-hipped stride and suave sheen of elegance, the man should have looked wrong in the dirty alley. Instead, Kace sensed the gloss was hiding something that felt very at home in the darkness.

"Rillian." Galen stepped forward. "Your timing is impeccable."

"I heard you had some trouble, Galen," the owner of the most exclusive casino in the District—the Dark Nebula—said. "I thought I'd see if you needed some assistance."

"Thank you," Galen said.

Rillian's black eyes fell on Rory. "Another of your women of Earth, I presume."

"My name is Rory," she said, her tone sharp. "And I belong to me."

The man's lips twitched and he inclined his head, his curious gaze running over her red hair. "A pleasure, Rory."

Kace tightened his hold on her. "We need to get her to safety."

"My security team will escort you home." Rillian looked at Rory again. "If you have an interest in visiting the District, Rory, my casino is always open."

Before she could respond, Kace turned her away. "I think she's had enough of the District today."

With Rillian's well-trained security team flanking them, Kace and the others moved out of the District, and into the back streets of Kor Magna's old town. This was where most of the city's local residents lived, worked, and played. Most locals avoided the District like the Noovian plague.

When he saw the cream stone walls of the arena rising up above them, Kace felt the first stab of relief. Rillian's team left them at the entrance to the arena, and Kace followed Galen and Raiden as they made their way through the tunnels. It wasn't until they stepped past the guards and through the huge double doors of the House of Galen, that he let himself really relax.

She was safe.

They headed straight for the living area, and Kace sat Rory down on one of the couches. Then, he patted down her arms, her sides, checking for any injuries. He saw no blood, no bruising.

"You want to check my teeth, too?" Her tone was as dry as the desert.

He ignored her. On the bottom of her shirt, he spotted a few flecks of blood. His brows drew together. "What's this blood?"

He jerked up the torn hem of her shirt. When she slapped at his hands, he gripped both her wrists with one hand.

The skin of her belly was covered in a dozen or so small nicks.

"It's just from some glass from the smashed windows. It's nothing."

Harper rushed into the room. "What happened?"

"We were attacked," Raiden told his woman. "Someone fired on us as we were leaving Zhim's apartment building."

Regan hurried in next, holding a small medical kit. "Everyone okay?"

Kace grabbed the kit, reached in and snatched up a tube of med gel. He rubbed some onto Rory's cuts.

They both went still for a second. Then he kept smoothing the gel onto her creamy skin.

"Ouch!"

"It's not bad," he said.

"Says you." She frowned at him. "Look, you're the one with a bullet lodged in your back. You need medical help, not me."

"Kace?" Galen asked. "You're wounded?"

"I'm aware of my body's limits, G. My body's already working to expel the projectile."

"So, who shot at you guys?" Harper asked.

"We don't know." Galen's tone turned icy cold. His anger like a blade.

"The shots came from the building across the street from where we were standing," Kace said. He'd instinctively noted everything he could about the situation.

Galen nodded. "I've already sent Lore and Nero

to take a look around."

"It must be someone with a beef against the House of Galen," Rory said.

"A beef?" Raiden asked, frowning.

Rory waved a hand. "A problem, a grudge?"

"No," Kace said.

He felt everyone looking at him.

Rory leaned forward. "What do you mean?"

He held her gaze. "Whoever fired on us, was aiming at you."

Chapter Four

Rory took two steps, the sand moving beneath her feet, and swung her sword.

The clang of metal echoed in the air around her, and she felt the blow reverberate through her arms. Damn, Harper packed a punch.

Rory stepped back, letting her sword drop. Her arms were so tired. She wiped an arm across her sweaty face.

"Come on, Rory. *Focus*," Harper said.

Gritting her teeth, Rory lifted her sword and attacked again. They'd been at it for a couple of hours, and Rory was determined to master the sword.

They moved back across the sand of the training arena. The clang of the swords was punctuated by their harsh grunts. A second later, Harper swung one of her swords hard. The force of the blow knocked Rory's sword out of her hand.

The training sword landed on the ground near some sparring dummies and Rory let out a frustrated noise. Right now, frustration was her constant companion.

"Dammit, Harper. You use two swords like a pro, and I can't even hold onto one."

Harper slid her swords into the scabbards at her hips. "I've been training with swords my whole life, plus, the last few months have been a pretty intense, advanced lesson. Give it time. You're strong and scrappy, you'll get it." Her friend moved closer, running a friendly hand across Rory's shoulder. "But this isn't really about the sword, is it?"

Rory nodded. The day had been full of questions, and not a single answer.

"You've had a pretty rough day today," Harper said. "Give yourself a break."

"Yeah." But the emotions churning in her gut were hot and angry. With a growl, Rory strode over to the closest sparring dummy and kicked it.

Not enough. She kicked it again. *Kick. Kick. Punch.*

"Ahh!" A hard roundhouse kick. This one set the dummy rocking.

Harper stopped beside her, her arms crossed over her chest. "You want to talk about it?"

Rory spun, lifting her hands to clasp them behind her head. "Where do I start? I'm still adjusting to life on a new planet. I miss my family. Someone is trying to kill me. I keep imagining Madeline in some house of horrors somewhere." Rory clenched her hands together, pushing back the memories. "And I'm lusting after an uptight gladiator."

Harper's mouth opened, then closed again.

Rory turned and gave the dummy another kick.

"So…Kace, huh?" Harper said slowly.

"I need a big, bossy gladiator like I need a hole in the head."

"He's a good man."

"Yes, but he's also a structured, military man. Have you seen the way he assesses everything? He never just reacts."

"That's what makes him so good in the arena." Harper stepped in front of Rory, drawing Rory's full attention. "Like I said, a good man, and one I think could do with a little shaking up."

Rory paused. She knew Harper pretty well and she heard what her friend wasn't saying. "But?"

"He's here temporarily, Rory. He's contracted here for two years, and he's already served six months. Once he finishes honing his skills in the arena, he'll go back to the military. Raiden's told me that Kace's planet, Antar, is dedicated to military life. They breed their people for it. For them, it's all about duty, honor, and protecting their world from their enemies."

Rory could see the duty, the honor, and the need to protect in him. Hell, she thought it was admirable. "I don't want to marry the guy, Harper."

"I know. But I don't want you hurt more than you already have been."

In an instant, all the fight went out of Rory. She moved over to her friend and gave Harper a hug. "I'm so glad you're here. And Regan, too." Rory lifted her head and looked around. "Speaking of which, where is Regan? I thought she'd nagged you to teach her how to use a sword."

Harper snorted. "We both know she's going to be

as good with a sword as she is at cards."

Rory smiled. Her sweet cousin lacked a killer instinct. Even as a kid, Regan was always growing plants and rescuing bugs. She couldn't even swat a fly.

"Anyway, I saw Thorin drag her off." Harper waggled her eyebrows. "Two guesses what they're up to."

Rory shook her head. To her, Thorin and Regan were like beauty and the beast. But they fit, and Rory had never seen Regan glow with happiness like she did now. Her strict parents had made Regan's life hell, and barely shown her any affection. Rory couldn't argue that big alien Thorin showered Regan in love.

Letting out a long breath, Rory stared at the sand. So while Harper and Regan were getting laid, and Rory was dreaming about it, Madeline was suffering. Something about all of it felt so wrong.

"We'll find Madeline." Harper gripped Rory's shoulder and squeezed. "Wherever she is, we won't leave her there." Then Harper looked over her shoulder. "Looks like your sexy, uptight gladiator found you."

Rory's head jerked up, and she saw Kace striding toward them.

He stood so straight and tall. As usual, he wore a beautiful leather arm guard over one shoulder, leaving all the rest of his muscles on display. Rory never tired of looking at him. The man was built.

She wanted to knock him down, jump on top of him, and lick every defined ridge on his chest and rock-hard stomach. She wanted to hear his groans of pleasure.

Damn. She shifted, feeling a flood of dampness between her legs. *Not now, Rory.*

"Staff training?" Kace asked.

Rory cocked a hip. "Good morning to you, too. I'm fine, thank you. As is Harper."

Kace frowned at her.

Harper coughed, although Rory was pretty certain the other woman was hiding a laugh.

"We're finished." She speared Rory with a look. "Do what makes you happy. We need a little pleasure to help cope with all the crap."

As Harper left, Rory found herself standing there with Kace.

"What did Harper mean?" Kace asked.

"Nothing. So, let's do this."

He led her over to the weapons rack at the edge of the training arena. "Someone tried to hurt you. You need to focus on protecting yourself."

His words were sobering. They moved along the display. There were shields, daggers, swords, and nets. And some things she didn't recognize. "Who makes all these?"

"Galen has a weapons-maker on staff," Kace said. "He makes some new weapons and deals with repairs. There is also a master weapons-maker here in Kor Magna, who sells to all the houses."

Rory ran her hand down the hilt of a longsword. "Any news on Madeline?"

"No."

She huffed out a breath. "Did Galen find out who shot at us?"

"No. By the time Lore and Nero reached the location, the shooter was long gone and didn't leave anything behind. We analyzed the projectile that hit me. It was generic, no identifying features."

"You're okay?"

He nodded. "Fully healed." He tilted his head. "Did you get some sleep last night?"

"A little." Not much. Not with memories of those projectiles slamming around them added to her nightmares. She shoved a hand through her hair. "Whoever did this can't be after me. Why kill me?"

"I don't know. But whoever it is, they won't get another chance." Kace's voice was hard and unyielding.

Rory felt something in her chest soften. She was used to fighting her own battles, but God, it was nice to know someone else was looking out for her.

Kace picked up a smaller staff from the rack. "I brought this out earlier. It's the right size for you."

He'd found it for her. She took the weapon, weighing it in her hands. It was made of a smooth, shiny metal, similar to Kace's staff. It was lighter than she'd imagined, and felt just right for her. As she moved it, the morning light caught on the carvings in the metal.

"It's Antarian writing," he told her. "The incantations of a warrior." He held up his own staff. Similar markings were etched on his staff. "With everything that's going on, it's very important you can defend yourself."

She nodded. "I'm pretty good with hand-to-hand—"

"It's better if you don't get that close. You're smaller and not as physically strong as every alien species here."

"You calling me small and weak?"

A faint smile moved his lips. "Weak is not a word that comes to mind when I think of you."

"You think of me?" She watched him steadily.

Something flickered in his blue eyes, then he straightened. "Come, let's go through some basic moves with the staff."

She released a breath and nodded. They moved out into the center of the arena, and found a space on the sand.

Kace started spinning his staff through the air with lethal, economic movements. He certainly wasn't elegant, there was too much discipline and power in his moves, but watching him was easy. He was a strong, athletic man at ease with his body and strength.

Rory positioned herself beside him and tried to mimic his movements. She swung the staff around, across, slicing through the air.

She pulled a few faces, trying to get the moves right. He added a few steps, and some new swings to the moves. His face was composed, calm, and untouched by everything around him. The perfect soldier.

Rory wanted a reaction. She wanted to see the passion that she was certain he was hiding under his cool façade.

"Okay, good," he said. "I think you've got the movements down. Let's try some basic sparring."

They faced each other, and when Kace moved in with a swing, she stepped up to counter it.

He showed her how to put the basic moves into action. She could see that he was holding back. It would be a while before she could really give him a workout with the staff.

But that didn't mean she was just going to keep it easy.

Studying the way he moved and attacked, she took a risk, sliding in under his arm. She got in close and whacked her staff into his side.

He grunted.

She stepped back, grinning at him. "Got you."

He frowned at her. "That was not a good move."

"But I got a hit in. Sometimes you need to do the unexpected, Kace."

His frown deepened, but he gestured for her to come at him again. They sparred some more, and, every now and then, she threw in one of her unexpected moves, sliding in close and jabbing him with an elbow or a kick to the leg.

A lot of the time, she just watched him. He used the staff like it was an extension of his body. God, she could watch the man do it all day.

On the next strike, she whirled around behind him, and pinched his ass.

As she pulled back laughing, Kace spun and glowered at her. The look on his face loosened the knot of tension in Rory.

"You are undisciplined," he bit out.

"Yep."

"We will continue until you master some restraint."

She swallowed another laugh. "We might be out here for a while, then."

He launched at her, and she barely got her staff up in time to block his hit. She spun away and came in again, the metallic thwacks of their staffs echoing across the arena.

"Good," Kace said. "Keep your elbow up."

His praise made her push harder. She got in under his arm and slid her body against his. She was going to try another punch, but he was already spinning to face her.

Rory leaped back. Three more strikes, both of them moving across the sand. When she got in close again, she slid her staff past his side until her body crashed into his—her front plastered to his rock-hard abdomen and sweaty chest.

Kace spun her, so fast she barely saw him move. He trapped her against him with his staff, her back pressed hard to his heaving chest. His staff rested against her ribs and the breath rushed out of her.

"I am a gladiator, Rory, and a soldier. It is best not to taunt me." His hot breath feathered over her ear.

She tilted her head back to look up at him. "What if I want to taunt you?"

His blue eyes flashed with desire so strong and potent it left her weak.

"Rory? Kace?" Galen's deep voice cut across the training arena.

They stayed pressed together for another second before Kace released her. Rory blinked, instantly missing the contact. He'd scrambled her brain and her hormones.

The imperator stopped a few meters away from them, his face its usual serious mask.

"I have word from Zhim."

Chapter Five

When they entered the living area, Kace saw all the others were already there, seated around the long table. He ushered Rory to a chair with a hand at the small of her back. Just that small bit of contact with her made his jaw clench.

He was feeling edgy, and couldn't find his usual calm. He wanted to blame the attack, but he knew he'd had this feeling from the moment he'd rescued Rory from the House of Vorn.

In the training arena, her teasing touches, the brushes of her lean, strong body…she was driving him out of his mind. He'd never met anyone like Rory Fraser before.

Galen turned toward a screen on the wall, and a second later it flickered to life. Zhim's face dominated. The information merchant was leaning forward toward the camera, and behind him, the room he was sitting in was jam-packed with screens full of scrolling images and text. The screens didn't appear to be in any sort of order and they were different sizes. The lack of order grated on Kace. This was clearly Zhim's inner sanctum.

"So," the information merchant started, "there are no contracts out on Rory's life."

Kace released a breath. That didn't make him feel much better. He'd prefer an enemy he could see coming. He studied her face. An enemy he could protect her from.

"And at first there wasn't even a whisper of your Madeline Cochran." Zhim sat back. "I thought maybe she wasn't even real. Now she's everywhere."

Kace frowned. He glanced at his fellow gladiators and saw they were all frowning, too. Rory was sitting up straight, watching Zhim intently, and holding her breath.

"What do you mean?" Galen demanded.

"I mean, there's a little here—" Zhim wiggled a hand "—and there's a little there—" another wiggle "—there's word of Madeline everywhere."

Rory slammed her fist on the table. "Just tell us, and quit the grandstanding."

Zhim focused on her, his expression turning serious. "I have reports coming in from all over the city. She has been spotted in the markets, the District, in the city backstreets…and that's just to name a few."

"Credible reports?" Kace asked.

"Yes, but something is clearly not right." Zhim's colored eyes sharpened. "Someone is playing a game with us. What I can tell you is that all of these reports are coming from reliable sources."

"Maybe someone's paying these people more than you do," Raiden suggested.

Zhim's tone darkened, the gleam of craziness gone. "These people would not cross me."

For the first time since he'd known the man, Kace saw something dangerous in the information merchant.

"All right," Galen said. "Send us the locations, and we'll check them out."

"Very well." Zhim nodded, and then the screen blinked off.

A moment later, Galen stared at a small, portable screen he had on the table. "Here it is." He studied the list and grunted. "I suggest we split up and each take a location. Find out if anyone really has seen Madeline, and who she was with. Harper and Raiden, head to the markets. Saff and Kace—"

"I'll go with Rory." Kace hadn't realized he was going to say that until the words came out, but he knew Rory wouldn't want to stay behind. And if she was going to step outside the House of Galen, he was going to be with her.

A muscle ticked in Galen's cheek. "It's best if Rory doesn't leave here—"

Rory abruptly stood. "This is my colleague we're talking about. I need to help find her. And I will not be locked up in here like an animal in a cage." She sat, her hands clamping down on the arms of her chair. "I've been caged, been chained, I've been locked up…I don't care if someone shoots at me again, as long as I'm free."

Galen stared at her. "Fine. Kace and Rory, you'll go to Aran's store off the main arena."

"Aran?" Rory asked.

"The arena's master weapons-maker," Kace told her.

"Thorin and Saff, head to the District, to—" Galen glanced at the screen again "—the Dragon Star Casino. Nero and Lore, you need to head down to the arena workers' living areas."

Everyone moved to head out. Kace grabbed his staff from where he'd rested it against the wall and turned to Rory. "Ready?"

She straightened. "Yes."

Kace strode over to a closet and pulled out a red-and-gray cloak. "I suggest you wear this. The symbol of the House of Galen will provide some protection." And it would cover those bare shoulders and arms that were driving him crazy. Not to mention the way her leather trousers cupped the gentle curves of her bottom.

She nodded and turned her back to him. She swept her hair up, revealing a slim neck. He stared at her creamy, smooth skin, and the vibrant red of her hair. His hands itched to touch.

You are not here to touch, Tameron. He secured the cloak, letting its folds fall around her body.

Moments later, they were heading out into the tunnels. They didn't have too far to go, and Kace strongly suspected that was why Galen had selected the weapons-master's store for Rory to check out. He had rooms just off the main arena.

The Kor Magna Markets offered many of the things that gladiators needed in the arena. But if you wanted the best weapons—the finest swords, the strongest staffs, the sharpest axes—you came to see Aran.

As they walked inside, Rory's eyebrows rose. "Wow."

The entire space was crowded with swords, staffs, and various other weapons. They were lined up on the walls, loaded on shelves and cabinets.

"Aran is known as the maker of the best weapons in this system. He sells to the gladiator houses as well as off-worlders."

She walked along a rack of swords, touching the metal hilts. "Some of these are beautiful."

Some were almost works of art, while others were plain and utilitarian, pretending to be nothing except what they were—dangerous weapons.

When she touched the sword at the end, its blade glowed and she snatched her hand back.

Kace moved closer to her. "The blade is enhanced with technology. Small machines—"

"Nano-tech." Her gaze sharpened. "What's it do?"

"Protects the metal. Cleans and repairs it. Enhanced weapons like these are not permitted in the arena."

A curtain at the back of the store parted and a tall, dark-skinned man ducked out of a room at the back. He straightened, his pale-gold gaze falling on them.

"The House of Galen pays me a visit," the weapons-maker said. "You do me an honor, Kace."

Kace inclined his head. "Greetings, Aran. I'm afraid we aren't here for weapons."

Aran's skin was as dark as space, and it was hard to guess his age. But Raiden had told Kace that Aran had been here well before Raiden had arrived, eighteen years ago. And he still looked exactly the same.

The big man crossed his bulging arms across his chest. "I don't have much else to offer, gladiator." His gaze dropped to Rory and then moved back to Kace. "You're sure you don't need weapons? I have some very small weapons that would fit her." He tilted his head, measuring Rory up. "She's very tiny."

Rory took a step forward. "I may be short, but you don't need to talk about me like I'm not here."

Kace looked toward the roof. "She also talks a lot."

She spun and pinned Kace with a glare. Over her shoulder, Kace saw Aran's mouth quirk into a smile.

"I can also hit…hard," she reminded him in a sweet voice he didn't buy for a second. She skewered Aran with a look and pointed at the enhanced sword. "I'd love to know how you add the nano-tech to the sword."

"Nano-tech?" the weapons-maker asked.

"The small machines—"

"Ah." Another faint smile. "Well, a weapons-maker never gives up his secrets."

Rory's gaze narrowed. "I can be very persuasive."

This time, Aran laughed. "That, I can believe." His gaze moved to Kace. "So, if you aren't after my weapons, how can I help you?"

"We're here to ask about a woman," Kace said.

"We heard that she was spotted here. She's small like Rory. They are from the same planet."

"She's got a compact build and dark hair cut to about here." Rory touched her jaw.

"She was possibly with Thraxians," Kace added.

A look of distaste crossed Aran's face. "I'm sorry. I haven't seen any Thraxians in here lately. They dislike paying for quality weapons." An edge crept into the man's voice. "And I haven't seen a tiny woman before you and your friend stepped in here."

Rory's shoulders sagged. "You're sure?"

He nodded. "I am good with details and never forget a face. I haven't seen your friend. I'm sorry. Believe me, I have no love for the Thraxian slavers. If I'd seen her, I would let you know."

Kace nodded his thanks. "If you do see her, could you contact the House of Galen?"

The weapons-maker nodded. "Of course."

"I'll be back to talk about that tech," Rory said.

Aran nodded. "You buy a weapon, and maybe I'll talk."

As they left the man's store, Kace watched Rory's friendly demeanor slip and she hunched her shoulders. She was usually vibrating with energy, ready to give as good as she got.

Now, she seemed empty.

"Rory—"

"She's being held captive." Green-and-gold eyes looked up at him, drowning in pain. "Hurt. Alone."

"Let's get back to the House of Galen. Maybe one of the others has had more luck than us."

"You know as well as I do that this is some game

the Thraxians are playing with us. We both know that no one has really seen her."

She was right, and Kace didn't know what to say to comfort her. He'd never really offered comfort to anyone. If they needed protection, or something killed, that he could do. But soothing hurts…that was beyond his skills.

As they got closer to the House of Galen, Rory's steps slowed. Finally, she stopped, staring at the entrance and the pair of guards standing beside it silently. "No. No." She shook her head and backed away. "Kace, I can't be locked in right now. I don't want to walk through those doors and have them slam shut behind me."

He heard the quiet desperation in her voice, and he hated that it was there. He hadn't known Rory long, but he knew she was fierce and tough. She'd hate this perceived weakness.

He held out a hand to her. "Come with me."

She didn't hesitate to put her hand in his. As he led her away from the House of Galen, and out of the tunnels and up into the stands of the arena, he realized that she'd put her trust in him.

On his planet, he was a commander and soldier. He was a hero of the Battle of Darron Valley. But Rory knew none of his illustrious reputation. Here, she was just trusting him, Kace the man, without question.

He reached a stairwell and led her up some stairs. There were a lot of them, but finally, they reached the top. He tugged her through one last door, bringing them out at the top of a tower that perched on one of the arena walls. Flags flapped in the wind, secured to the peak.

The desert wind caught Rory's hair, tossing her curls around her face. It didn't quite offer the view that Zhim's penthouse did, but the sight of the sprawling city below was still stunning. It was one of Kace's favorite places to come when he needed some time alone.

Rory moved to the stone railing and leaned out over it. He realized she wasn't paying any attention to the view. Her eyes were closed and she pulled in a deep breath.

He watched her, realizing he could actually see the tight tension flow from her body. He was reminded of just how tired she looked.

"Thank you." She turned to look at him. "Sometimes, when I worked on the space station, I would have given anything to feel the wind on my face." She looked up at him, something unreadable in her eyes. "I like open spaces, I like feeling free."

"You need to get some sleep."

She shot him a sad smile. "I wish." She took another deep breath. "I guess since my rescue, I hadn't realized I was still feeling so...hemmed in."

"It is normal to feel that way, Rory."

She nodded. "But Harper and Regan haven't. They love being at the House of Galen. And I do, too, but sometimes..."

"The walls close in around you."

She cocked her head. "You feel that way, too?"

"Sometimes. I've spent most of my life around my fellow soldiers, without much privacy. I never realized how much I enjoyed some time alone until I came here."

She took a step toward him, and then another. Kace's muscles locked and he found he couldn't move away. She reached up and pressed her palms against his chest. As her fingers moved across his skin, he saw need flare in her eyes. He felt a matching desire ignite in his gut.

"I don't feel trapped when I'm with you," she murmured.

Her fingers brushed across his nipples and he sucked in a hard breath, his pulse spiking.

"Rory…"

"I'm right here."

He grabbed her wrist and held it. He stood there, trapped between his duty and his own desires.

***

She could feel the coiled tension in Kace's body. He was wound tight.

God, she wanted this serious, locked-down man so much.

Rory went up on her toes and kissed him. As her lips moved over his, he didn't move, but against her chest, she felt his heart hammering behind his ribs.

She went back down, eyeing his hard chest. All those glorious muscles. She pressed a kiss to the center of all that bronze skin. Then she bit him. It wasn't hard, but damn, she wanted to sink her teeth into him.

His body jolted and a sound tore from his throat, then his hands shot up and grabbed her arms. "I'm not here for pleasure."

"But you want me, don't you?"

Silence.

She pressed her palms against his chest, felt his muscles tighten under her touch. "You like my hands on you?"

His breathing was ragged, his face stark. "Yes. But it doesn't change anything."

"What are you here for?" she asked quietly.

"To increase my skills as a soldier. For duty and honor. They are valued above all else on my planet."

"You aren't allowed to feel any pleasure?" She moved closer, and accidentally brushed the large bulge in the front of his trousers.

They both groaned.

Then a thought occurred to her. "Have you...been with a woman before?"

A jerky nod. "The military provide women on our scheduled breaks."

Jesus. Rory tried to sort through it all. Kace had never had sex with a woman of his choice. A woman who wasn't paid to spend time with him.

"Do you want to touch me, Kace?"

He stared down at her, pressing into her body.

"I want to touch you," she murmured. "So much. I have since you helped rescue me."

His big body shuddered against her. "Yes. Yes, I want to touch you."

They both moved. He yanked her upward and

Rory wrapped her legs around his hips. His mouth came down on hers. The kiss wasn't rough. He was almost cautious, at first. Then she opened her mouth, dipping her tongue in for a taste of him. He growled and deepened the kiss.

Kace moved forward, backing her up, until Rory felt the stone wall against her back. He ground his hips against her, the hard length of his cock pressing against where she was wet, and hot, and empty.

The kiss turned wilder, Kace finding his rhythm. He was drinking her in, his tongue delving inside her mouth, like he needed the taste of her to survive. She slid her hands up into his hair and kissed him back.

When he lifted his head, both of them were panting. She licked her swollen lips. "More. Please."

His hands slid up under her shirt, and he pushed the fabric up. His gaze was glued to her small breasts. His huge hands cupped them, his fingers flicking over her nipples. One hand slid down beneath her and he pushed her upward until her breasts were eye-level with his face. Then he leaned forward.

He sucked one nipple into his mouth and she moaned. As her body jerked against him, her hands pulled roughly at his hair.

She rubbed herself against him, desperate for something to ease the growing need inside her. Involuntarily, her hips started moving, sliding along that ripped abdomen and the bulge of his cock. Sensations shot through her, and she kept rubbing against him.

"You frustrate me," he ground out the words against her breasts. He moved one hand down, clamping on her hip to keep her rocking against him. "You tempt me beyond reason, Rory."

"I don't mean to." Her words turned into a long drawn out moan.

His hands tightened on her, and he slowed the movements of her hips.

"Don't stop." If he stopped, Rory thought she might die.

But then he shifted her until her legs were clamped around one of his hard thighs. He started moving her, so she was riding his thigh. Each move sent a jolt against her clit. Her hands jerked in his hair, and she slid them down to his arms. Sensations powered through her body. She could feel her orgasm growing, looming over her like a wave.

"Look at me," he growled.

Her gaze jerked up and was caught by the fierce glow of his blue eyes. Another hard rub on his muscled thigh and she splintered apart. Pleasure drowned her and she cried out.

Kace held onto her as she came back to reality. Her head dropped to his shoulder, small tremors still rocking her body. Her fingers were buried in his hard biceps, and she could feel his gaze on her.

God, she wanted to touch him. She wanted to tear his clothes off and take him inside her body. More than anything, she wanted to feel connected to him, feel him moving inside her. Then he lowered her until her feet touched the stone floor.

For a second, Rory wasn't sure if she'd be able to stand up, but she locked her knees. Kace stepped away from her, and when she looked up, his face looked like it was carved from stone.

Her stomach dropped. He didn't look like a man with loving on his mind.

"I'm not here for this," he said again, his words encased in ice.

Rory wrapped her arms around her middle. She felt horribly exposed and alone. "I want you, Kace, and you want me…there's nothing wrong with that."

"We can't do this, Rory. I can't split my focus. My loyalties lie with my people."

God, she'd just humped an alien gladiator who clearly didn't want her as much as she wanted him. Could her life get any worse? "Okay, look—"

"And you are in danger, which means right now, I need to focus on your safety. As a member of the House of Galen, I will ensure you don't get hurt."

Well, that made her feel pretty unimportant. "I—"

"If you need release, I suggest you find someone else," Kace said.

The words peppered her skin like bullets, and made her flinch. Drawing herself up, Rory pulled the last dregs of her pride around herself. "I hear you loud and clear, gladiator. And maybe I will find someone else."

She turned and walked away without waiting for him.

Chapter Six

It was almost fight time.

Kace once again stood in the tunnel, waiting to be called out into the arena. He reached over and tightened the straps on his arm guard. The leather was molded perfectly to his body, and decorated with Antarian etchings. Trying to find his usual calm, he traced a design of a stylized flower with three petals that was etched into the leather—an ancient symbol of the Creators, who'd seeded life on the planets throughout the galaxy.

It didn't help. He'd been here so many times—waiting for a fight—and usually, he was focused and ready.

But tonight, he felt unsettled. Off.

All he could think about was the taste of Rory, the feel of her slim, strong body against him, and the husky sounds of her cries as she found her pleasure.

He hissed out a breath, his hands tightening on his staff.

"What's wrong with you?" Saff stepped in front of him, eyeing him with a narrowed gaze.

"Nothing."

He heard the sound of the crowd outside

intensifying. They were pumped and ready for the show.

"You're edgy and unfocused." Saff was frowning. "It's not like you."

He knew Saff had some telepathic abilities—not that he'd ever been aware of her using them. He wondered if she could pick up on his emotions. "Just thinking about whoever took shots at us. And finding Madeline Cochran."

"No you're not."

"Leave it, Saff."

"Hey." She touched his arm. "I'm on your side, military man. You go out there without your head in the right space, you'll get hurt. For some strange reason, I like you in one piece."

She was his friend, and she always had his back. He took a deep breath. "I'm fine. When we step onto the sand, I'll be focused."

She watched him for another beat, then rolled her eyes. "Men."

Suddenly, the hum of engines filled the tunnel. He turned and saw a sleek line of combat chariots coming down the tunnel.

Tonight was to be a chariot fight.

The chariots were all identical, all made of a silver-gray metal, and they hovered just off the ground. The four vehicles pulled to a stop. Galen drove the lead chariot, followed by Thorin, then the chariot engineer Galen employed. Kace blinked. Rory was driving the final chariot.

Kace's shoulders tensed. He hadn't seen her since he'd trailed her back to the House of Galen yesterday, after their moment in the tower.

After she'd learned that all the other sightings of Madeline had been false leads as well, she'd gone to her room. Kace had wanted to go to her at countless points throughout the night, but...

He pulled his staff closer, staring blindly at the Antarian markings. Love wasn't something Antarians believed in. It didn't exist. Procreation came through planned pairings of the strongest individuals. Most of the time, those pairs didn't even know each other.

Love was just a loss of control, brought on by rampaging hormones. A chemical imbalance.

Rory leaped out of the chariot, holding her toolbox in one hand. When Kace saw what she was wearing, he stiffened. *What the drak?*

Tight leather trousers slicked over her legs, and her deep-green halter top fastened behind her neck, but to him it looked like not much more than a small triangle of fabric that left her slim shoulders bare.

"What are you doing here?" he demanded.

She shot him a cool look. "Galen asked me to work with Jarno." She nodded at the grizzly old chariot engineer. "I'm learning how to maintain the chariots." She lifted her chin. "And then I'm going to head up to the stands to watch the fight, have a few drinks, and find someone to have some fun with." She turned away.

Kace blinked, staring at her back. Apart from a few tiny strings, her shirt left her skin bare—delicate shoulder blades and more enticing freckles on display. His hands clamped down hard on his staff. He knew exactly what "fun" meant. The thought of anyone putting his hands on her, kissing her… Kace was surprised the metal didn't buckle under his hands.

"Oh, now I know what your problem is." Saff shook her head. "Another gladiator falling for the charms of an Earth girl."

"You know I'm not here to fall for anyone."

"Right. You're here to be the perfect soldier." Saff shook her head.

"My people don't believe in forming romantic relationships."

Saff made a sound. "Your people train babies from birth not to connect, to be able to head into a fight and not be bothered by pesky emotions."

He looked over at Rory again. She was laughing, and even had crusty Jarno laughing. Jarno never laughed. Lore, too, was standing close, looking over her shoulder with a smile.

She drew people in. Kace resisted the urge to slam his fist into the tunnel wall.

"Yet another casualty," Saff muttered. "Even if you are being stubborn about it."

"Enough, Saff." He used the same tone that he'd used on misbehaving soldiers.

The female gladiator threw her hands up. "Drop it. Got it. But for the record, I like her. I think she'd shake you up a bit."

Raiden stepped forward. "Time to go."

Kace climbed into the closest chariot with Saff. Ahead, he watched Harper and Raiden claim the lead chariot. Thorin was fighting with a new recruit this evening, and Lore and Nero were in the rear chariot.

Rory appeared beside Kace's vehicle. "We did some work on the steering mechanism of this one today. It was tugging to the left. Any problems, let us know."

Kace nodded.

She hesitated. "Good luck out there, pretty boy."

As she turned and walked away, Kace couldn't drag his eyes away from the gentle sway of her slim hips and the bare skin of her back.

***

Rory found her seat beside Regan and settled in. Tonight, Harper was fighting, and Rory was excited to watch her friend.

"They all set?" Regan asked.

Rory nodded. "They're fearless." Kace had looked so strong and sure, waiting to head into the arena.

She saw the chariots roar in, to the appreciation of a noisy crowd, doing a circle around the arena floor. The vehicles were amazing, and she couldn't wait to learn more about how their propulsion systems worked. Jarno knew every inch of them. He'd been less than enthusiastic when Galen had first introduced them, but after she'd asked about a thousand questions, and clearly been interested in the inner workings of the chariots, he'd warmed up. She'd even gotten a laugh or two out of him.

The crowd started chanting the gladiators'

names. She glanced up at the tiers of seats and the thousands of spectators. They were completely spellbound.

The shouting got louder. She glanced back at the floor and saw the chariots of the opposing gladiators enter from a tunnel on the opposite side of the arena.

She leaned forward. “Who are they fighting tonight?”

“The House of Felis,” Regan said. “The furry ones.”

Like most of the gladiator houses, the fighters weren’t all of one species, but she easily spotted the tall gladiators in the lead chariot. Their bodies were covered in a tan-colored fur. They had elongated snouts, and sharp-pointed ears, that gave them a vaguely feline look. One had small, high, fur-covered breasts, so Rory guessed she was female, even though she was the same size as her fighting partner.

The fight siren sounded, wailing out across the arena.

Harper and Raiden’s chariot veered across the arena, drawing in close to the lead Felis chariot. Harper was driving. The two chariots sped along and Rory watched as they bumped into each other. Harper pulled back a little and Raiden leaned out, his sword glinting in the lights of the arena.

Next, Kace and Saff raced past. She watched Kace swinging his staff. Then he jumped up, standing on the side wall of his chariot.

Damn. Rory’s mouth dried. What the hell was he

doing? He reached across the gap, striking at the opposing gladiators.

His balance was perfect, that handsome face focused and disciplined. She admired that about him, even when it drove her crazy.

Stop thinking about him. He'd made it clear that while he was attracted to her, he didn't want to be.

The next chariot sped by, containing Thorin and a tall, reptilian gladiator, who was tossing a net at a Felis chariot. Last, Lore and Nero roared past. Lore was driving with flair, zigzagging over the sand and cutting off the rival chariot beside them. Nero was fighting with hard, unforgiving blows of his sword.

As they circled around again, Rory watched as Raiden knocked one of his opponents out of his chariot. The Felis gladiator tumbled out onto the sand with the cry. The crowd roared.

Regan cheered and bumped her hip against Rory.

"You know, I never thought this would be your kind of thing," Rory said.

"I never thought I'd like watching fights, either." Regan tucked some blonde hair back behind her ear. "But there's just something about it..."

"Something wild? Primal? Gets the blood pumping?"

Regan nodded, a flash of color on her cheeks. "It's electrifying. Especially when I watch Thorin fighting."

Rory had done some amateur MMA bouts back on Earth. She understood the appeal of this kind of event. She'd been there, pitting herself against someone, fighting to win.

As Saff and Kace came close again, Kace was still balanced on the chariot's edge. He shouted something to Saff and the female gladiator grinned and moved their chariot closer to their opponents.

Kace bent his knees. What was he doing? He leaped into the air, flying across the gap.

Rory's heart lodged in her throat and, almost as one, the crowd gasped.

He landed in the other chariot, slamming into the passenger. It was too tight for him to use his staff, so instead, he landed solid hits and punches. The Felis gladiator fought back hard.

Kace dodged some blows, the two of them twisting and turning in the tight space. Then Kace gripped the gladiator's furred chest, spun again and tossed the male out into the sand.

As the crowd cheered, so did Rory.

She watched as Kace turned to the driver. This gladiator was female and she wasn't Felis. She had copper-colored skin, and a thick, dark braid that reached her waist. Lots of beaten metal bracelets banded her arms and neck.

She looked up at Kace, trembling. He lowered his arms and held a hand out to her.

She looked at it for a second, then took it. Kace tugged her to his side and took over driving the chariot.

The woman had conceded.

Rory glanced at the other chariots, and saw the House of Galen had taken down all the Felis gladiators.

The fight was over.

She watched the House of Galen gladiators move their chariots into a victory lap of the ring. As the train of vehicles passed the House of Galen seats, Rory saw the female gladiator gazing up at Kace adoringly, pressing into his side. Rory dimly heard the announcers declaring the House of Galen the winners.

Rory swallowed, even as sparks flared in her blood. She *hated* seeing another woman touching Kace. She really wasn't known for her even temper.

She'd always fought for what she wanted. With three older brothers, she'd had to. Especially when she'd wanted to study engineering and complete her MMA training. She was not a quitter.

Kace looked up at her, and she felt the electric connection between them.

She wasn't going to let him ignore whatever arced between them. *The fight is on, gladiator.* She winked at him.

"Ready for the party?" Regan said.

Rory looked at her friend. "Party?"

"The sponsors always invite the gladiators up to the corporate box. Usually, they don't go, and just prefer a few drinks back in the living quarters. But tonight, Galen has said everyone needs to make an appearance. From what I hear, this sponsor's parties can get a bit…wild."

Wild was good. It suited her mood tonight. Rory nodded. "Sounds like fun."

"Great. We'll head up. Harper, Raiden, Thorin,

and the others will shower and meet us there."

When they entered the party, it took Rory's eyes a second to adjust. The lights were low, the room was packed with people, and the throb of music was loud. She saw a feast of food and drinks laid out.

Then her gaze widened. Servers moved through the room, their long, sinuous bodies naked except for a covering of glittery silver and red paint. Several dancers painted in the same colors writhed on poles on a small stage.

"Wow," Rory murmured.

"Let's get a drink."

Soon they were seated at the bar watching the bartender pour elaborate, layered drinks into long glasses. The partygoers erupted into cheers and applause.

Rory looked over and saw the gladiators had arrived.

There was a small group of lower-ranked gladiators who eagerly joined the party. Harper and Raiden came in behind them. They both had wet hair, and Rory could guess what they'd been up to. Raiden pulled Harper into his arms, pressing a hard kiss to her lips.

God, it made Rory's belly tight just watching them. The way that man worshipped everything about Harper made Rory insanely envious. She saw Kace step in behind them. He was watching the couple as well.

His hair was damp and his shirt didn't cover much, leaving his arms and most of his chest bare.

Damn him for looking so delicious.

Thorin barged in and cut a straight path to Regan. He dropped onto a stool beside them and tugged Regan onto his lap. He nuzzled his face into the side of her neck while she stroked his short hair.

Another pang of envy hit Rory.

"Nice moves, military man." Saff's voice carried as she bumped her shoulder against Kace's.

"Hell yeah." Thorin reached out and slapped Kace on the back.

Kace nodded. "It was a good fight."

"Let's celebrate." Lore strode closer with a pretty blonde woman hanging on his arm. She shot the gladiator a sultry smile. "Thought we were going to need the healers to remove that female gladiator from you, Kace."

Rory tasted a sour taste in her mouth and snatched up her colored drink.

Kace's gaze flicked her way. "Yes, she was...persistent."

Rory took a large swig of the multi-colored liquid. Was he talking about her or that darn Felis gladiator?

Lore shoved a drink into Kace's hand and the gladiators all started to relax. Rory realized it must take a while for them to come down from the high of the fight. Rory sipped her drink again, letting the burn of the alcohol and the beat of the unfamiliar music lull her. It was nice to be a part of this group and remember that she was no longer alone.

"You were amazing tonight."

The purred words made her look over. A curvy woman with a painted face was running her hands up Kace's chest.

Regan had called these women arena flutterers. They made no pretenses about the fact they enjoyed sex with gladiators. Rory got the impression most of the gladiators were only too happy to take them up on their offers. Across the room, Lore had his arms full with two women. There were also plenty of lower-ranked gladiators making the most of the party.

Rory sipped her drink again. She actually sort of admired the flutterers. They knew what they wanted and they went after it.

She wanted to look away, but she made herself watch Kace and the woman. He gently grabbed her wrists and pushed her away.

"Thanks." He turned her and pointed to where Nero was leaning against the bar nursing an ale. "You might have more luck with him."

The woman cocked her head, her gaze running over Nero's big body. "Okay. Thanks."

As she sauntered off, Kace turned his head. His gaze locked with Rory's and she felt the hairs on her arms rise.

He stalked toward her.

Chapter Seven

As Kace leaned against the bar beside Rory, she breathed in the clean, freshly-showered scent of him. "I enjoyed the chariot fight tonight."

He nodded, his big body taut. She wished she knew what he was thinking. She just wanted to see him relax and enjoy himself.

She looked past him to where four painted dancers—two men and two women—were grinding against each other on the small stage. "This is pretty wild."

"It'll get a lot wilder as the night wears on," he said.

Silence fell again and Rory desperately wanted to reach out and touch him.

Galen appeared. "Make sure you do a few rounds. Talk with the sponsors."

Kace scowled. "Sure."

The imperator's gaze fell on Rory. "They are pretty interested in you too, Rory."

"Me?" Her eyebrows rose.

"You're from an unknown planet, and your small stature and red hair are unique."

Kace's hand curled around the bar. "You want to parade her around."

Galen's gaze turned icy. "No. I want her to talk to a few people, smile, and have a good time. The people here pay a lot of money to the House of Galen. That feeds and clothes us all." With that, the imperator strode off.

"He seems tense," Rory noted.

Kace shrugged. "Out of everyone, Galen hates these parties the most. He just knows they are a necessary evil."

A group of well-dressed ladies wearing gold half-masks moved past, whispering and giggling. Rory stared at them. "What's with the masks?"

"They are wealthy women who come to…sample the gladiators."

Rory choked on her drink. "What?"

"Some of the gladiator houses take money so wealthy patrons can have sex with gladiators. The women prefer to keep their identities secret."

"Does Galen…?"

Kace smiled. "No, even Galen draws the line at whoring out his gladiators."

Rory stirred a straw in her drink. "I see now you get lots of…offers from women."

Kace stayed quiet, his gaze on her.

She shrugged a shoulder. "I guess I realize now that my attraction to you is just another offer in a long line. I'm sorry if—"

He grabbed her chin and she squeaked. He lifted her face until her gaze met his.

"You will not compare us to anything that goes on in this room."

Her mouth parted. His gaze was so intense, she

felt stripped bare. "Kace…"

He muttered a curse and released her. His face tensed, and she could read the battle in every line of his body.

He gave her a stiff nod. "Enjoy the rest of the party."

Suddenly, even in a party full of people, Rory felt very alone.

***

The music changed, the wild sounds of strings filling the room.

Kace tried to relax. He'd found himself the quietest, darkest part of the room and stood there, carefully sipping his drink. And fighting to keep from looking at Rory.

When he'd first joined the House of Galen, he'd avoided the after-fight celebrations. He'd always gone back to his room and forced himself to go over military texts. He'd told himself not to get used to the excesses of the arena.

But slowly, over time, he'd realized that bonding with his fellow gladiators was just as important as actually fighting in the arena. The more time they spent together, the better their rapport on the sand. And, he had finally come to admit that he liked spending time with his friends.

Rory was still at the bar and he was sorry that where before she'd looked happy and relaxed, she now looked as tense as he did.

Why was he so drawn to her? He knew he

couldn't claim her the way he wanted, so he had to stay away from her.

All around them, people were having fun. The guests were fawning over all the gladiators present, drinking, and dancing.

He watched a well-dressed man approach Rory. He was tall and slender, dressed in royal blue trousers and a tunic edged in gold. Kace was too far away to hear their conversation, but Rory smiled and nodded. The man slid onto the stool beside her.

Kace scowled and wished he could hear what the man was saying. From the way he was dressed, Kace guessed he was a sponsor, and Kace didn't like that at all. Most of the sponsors he knew were wealthy and believed they should get everything—and anyone—they wanted.

Rory and the man were in an animated conversation. Whatever they were discussing, it lit up her face. The man was fiddling with something and Rory asked to see it. Kace frowned. A coin, maybe.

Kace slammed his glass down on a side table. If the guy got any closer to her, he was going to go over there and…

Regan appeared beside Rory, dragging a clearly reluctant Harper with her. As the two women tugged Rory toward the dance floor, Kace relaxed a little.

Then he found himself flanked by Raiden and Thorin.

"Regan wanted to dance," Thorin said. "Something about being alive and celebrating."

"Harper did not want to dance." Raiden sipped his drink. "She said something about preferring to be thrown out an airlock."

"She appears to be enjoying herself now," Kace noted.

He watched the three Earth women swaying their hips. Their dancing was completely different to the gyrations of the painted dancers. Rory laughed, raising her arms above her head and shimmying against Regan.

Harper warmed up and soon the three women were moving to the beat, completely unaware that every male in the room was watching them.

"Drakking hell." Raiden tossed back his drink. "I didn't know Harper could move like that."

"I'm making Regan do a private dance for me later." Thorin's gaze was glued to the small woman.

Kace couldn't take his eyes off Rory. She slid down in a crouch before sliding back up, her back arched. She pulsed with life and he wanted to grab her and never let go. Absorb that light and energy, bask in it.

Regan bopped over to the musicians and after a lot of talking and hand waving, she crossed back to her friends. The music changed to a jaunty beat that sounded completely different to the Enkan music playing earlier.

The Earth women let out screams and threw their arms in the air, hips swinging. All three of them were singing and smiling.

Thorin frowned. "They're singing something about being afraid and petrified, but growing strong." He smiled. "They're singing about surviving. That as long as they have love—" The big man shook his head.

"To the remarkable women of Earth." Raiden lifted his drink.

The song ended, but the women kept dancing. A moment later, both Raiden and Thorin stiffened.

"No," Raiden growled, stalking toward the dance floor, Thorin right behind him.

Kace saw that three big off-worlders had converged on the women. The men had glossy, oiled chests and flowing hair. They pressed in close to Rory and the others.

Raiden pulled Harper off the dance floor while Thorin allowed himself to be talked into a dance. The big gladiator scowled at the off-worlders, while Regan pressed herself against him, dancing as he mostly stayed still.

Two of the off-worlders pushed up against Rory. She was grinning, shimmying with them. Letting them run their hands over her. She looked tiny sandwiched between the men.

No. Kace strode over and clamped a hand on the closest man's shoulder. He jerked him away from Rory.

"Go," Kace told the man. "Or I'll break your arm."

"Kace!" Rory cried.

"Are you his?" the second man asked her.

She stared at Kace and swallowed. "No. No, I'm not."

The off-worlder stepped closer to her. “You have no—”

Kace yanked Rory to his side. “Go now, or I will hurt you.”

Something in his tone got through. With unhappy scowls, the men moved away. Kace swung Rory around. “What did you think you were doing?”

“Dancing.”

He growled.

Rory pushed a hand through her hair. “I guess I was being an idiot. I wanted you to notice me.”

Kace went still. “You succeeded.”

She pressed her hands to his chest. “Well, since you scared off my dance partners, you’ll have to dance with me.”

“I don’t dance.”

“Then you shouldn’t have intervened.”

He stiffened. “You wanted them touching you?”

“You know what I want, you stubborn man. Now be quiet and dance.” She pressed into him, swaying.

Kace couldn’t make himself leave. He wrapped his arms around her and absorbed the feel of her.

“What were you talking to the man at the bar about?” he demanded.

“What man?”

“The sponsor.”

“Malix?”

Kace pulled her up on her toes. “You were engrossed, absorbed by him.”

“And you didn’t like that?” she asked quietly.

“No.”

"Kace, you're leaving me so confused."

"What. Were. You. Talking. About?"

"His company makes spaceships. We were talking about engineering and his wife, husband and kids, who he misses when he travels. His planet has committed triads. God, two people in a relationship is hard enough, imagine three."

Kace relaxed a little. "He gave you something."

"This?" She pulled out a coin with a symbol on it. It looked like a stylized lightning bolt. "He said someone had given it to him."

"It doesn't look like the usual currency here on Carthago."

"Malix said it was nothing important. An invitation to a party or something. He said people are always trying to curry his favor and inviting him to places. He didn't want it and I thought it looked pretty."

The last of Kace's tense muscles relaxed.

"You realize you're jealous, right?"

He stopped and stared down at her. Antarians did not feel jealousy. Jealousy implied strong emotions and strong attachment.

Rory's gaze went over his shoulder and her eyes widened. "Oh, my God. Are they…?"

He turned and saw the painted dancers on the stage were doing a different kind of dance. A woman was on her knees, sucking the cock of the man standing in front of her, while another man was taking her from behind.

Rory scanned the room. Kace saw her taking in others on the dance floor with hands up skirts and trousers loosened. In the shadows at the edge of the room came the raw sounds of flesh slapping against flesh.

Her hands tightened on his shirt, her gaze coming back to the painted dancers on stage. She was watching the woman swallowing the man's cock as he rocked his hips forward.

Instantly, Kace imagined himself and Rory. Rory with her hands pressed against his thighs, her mouth stretched wide as she sucked his cock past her pink lips.

"Harper and Raiden are waving at us from the door." Rory's voice was husky. "I guess we can leave now."

Kace nodded and stepped back, breaking the spell. He kept a distance between them as they joined the others and made it back to the living quarters at the House of Galen.

Another round of drinks was passed around, and here, in their home, he saw his friends truly relax. He watched Rory talking with Nero, remembering those heated moments on the dance floor. He watched his friends enjoy themselves, and found his gaze straying to Raiden and Harper, and Thorin and Regan.

It was an unpleasant reminder of things he couldn't have.

Things he suddenly wanted desperately.

He shot to his feet and set his glass down. He strode out of the room.

As he walked into the corridor, he decided he'd go down to the gym and work out some of this tension.

In the gym, the lights clicked on automatically. He glanced over and stared briefly at the light that Rory had fixed the other night.

Rory. Rory was all he could think about.

He stood there, in the center of the space, his blood pumping thickly through his veins. The edginess made him feel like hitting something.

He turned to the gel-filled bags hanging from the ceiling. He tore off the shirt he'd pulled on after his shower and started punching the closest bag. He slammed his fists into it, waiting to find that control he'd depended on his entire life.

The sound of light footsteps caught his ears. He knew who it was, and he didn't look up. He kept torturing the bag.

"Stop, Kace," Rory said quietly.

"Go away," he growled.

"No."

Chapter Eight

Kace dropped his hands, fighting the urge to grab her. His harsh breathing was loud in the silent space.

Rory moved in behind him. He felt her hands on his back, like the brush of feather-light wings, and then she pressed a kiss to the center of his back.

He shuddered. "You keep pushing."

"I'm not doing anything, Kace, except letting you know I like you."

"I don't want to hurt you, Rory."

"How could you hurt me?"

He turned. She was so close and those freckles teased him, begging him to count each one. "Love doesn't exist on my planet. I've never seen it or felt it. Romantic relationships are forbidden. Sex is tolerated. They are all things that can get in the way of being a good soldier."

She gasped. "You aren't allowed to love?"

"No, Rory, I don't believe in love."

"I don't believe you."

Rory's words made Kace's gut churn. "What?"

"I've seen the way you watch Harper and Raiden. With envy in your eyes." She lifted her stubborn chin. "I've seen the way you watch me."

They stared at each other, no other sound in the room. Kace told himself to walk out, to leave, but his feet refused to move.

Rory Fraser was like a vortex, pulling him in.

She let out a small sigh. "I think we both need to work out some of the tension." She pulled away and kicked off her shoes. "Let's spar."

Kace was certain this wasn't a good idea, but he still couldn't make himself walk away.

She wandered over to a wall of weapons and pulled off two short fighting sticks. They were made of well-worn wood.

"I know you're a master with the staff, but have you used fighting sticks, as well?" She held one out.

He took the light stick and nodded. The stick was far shorter than his staff, and used in a completely different way.

"I've done some sayoc stick grappling at home." She spun the stick in an experienced move, holding it up over her shoulder. "What I like about it is that size doesn't matter, skill does."

She came at him.

Kace moved his stick, meeting hers. They traded a rapid combination of strikes, their sticks smacking against each other. He found himself moving back across the mats as she drove him backward with skilled, lightning-fast moves of her stick.

She was good. Very good.

Concentrating, Kace watched her style and timed the arcs of her stick. But she varied her attacks, and he had to use every bit of his skill to block her.

She pulled back, half crouched, and they circled each other on the mats.

"Come on, Kace. Attack."

He shook his head. "I won't hurt you."

Something moved in her eyes. "No, of course you won't. You're too noble, too protective. A hero."

"Hardly. I was born and bred to fight. Antarian children are sent to military school at age three."

She dropped her hands, her stick by her side. "Your family?"

"No families, Rory. There haven't been family units on Antar for centuries. It was more efficient for children to be schooled straightaway. It was decided that family attachments promote emotional ties. Emotions make you weak."

"That's insane. Emotions can make you stronger, as well. Give you something to fight for."

"We fight for honor. For our people."

"That's not the same as fighting to protect the people you love." She shook her head. "Why would your people choose to do this?"

"We've been fighting with a species from a neighboring system for most of our history. Over time, the war shaped my planet. For an Antarian soldier, the pinnacle of success in life is serving our planet and battling the Hemm'Darr aliens."

"What about children who aren't suited to fighting? What about children who show talent in other areas? Artists, doctors, engineers?"

"Everyone works for the military. People's skills are matched to certain roles."

He saw sympathy flash in her eyes.

Her hands tightened on her stick. "What about what *you* want?"

"I want to serve my people."

"That's because you've been brainwashed to think that from birth." She huffed out a breath. "That can't be it, can it, Kace? You have more to offer."

Her words forced an itchy, uncomfortable feeling to crawl through his chest. "Enough. Are we fighting?"

He lunged at her, swinging his stick.

She spun and ducked. He'd barely turned around when she came at him. Her stick thwacked against his shoulder, and as he gritted his teeth, she kicked him in the side.

Like a Gorran wraith, she moved again, fast and fluid. Her stick struck his lower back and she turned again, the stick slapping his thigh.

He grunted. *Enough.* He rushed at her, wrapped his arms around her hips, and tackled her to the mats.

He heard the air rush out of her, and both their fighting sticks slapped the mats. He was too big and heavy to stay on top of her. He rolled to the side, but she moved with him. With a lithe move of her legs and arms, he suddenly found himself held in a head lock. She wrapped herself around him like an Antarian constrictor serpent.

Kace shoved against her hold, and felt her muscles shaking as she strained to hold him.

But he knew he was stronger. He shoved again

and broke her hold. They rolled across the mats, and this time he pinned her beneath him.

He expected to see angry eyes. Instead, she laughed.

He looked down at her, at this bright, vibrant woman with her unique red hair and those fascinating spots across her nose.

Then she leaned up and pressed her mouth to where his neck and shoulder joined. She nipped his skin, catching a tendon between her teeth.

Instantly, Kace's cock went hard, pressing against her softness. The air turned hot and charged.

He had to have her. He needed something.

Slamming his mouth against hers, he drank her in. She jerked against him, her mouth opening. He slid his tongue inside and she met him, tongues dueling.

"Yes, Kace." She peppered his chin with kisses, her hands sliding into his hair. "God, you turn me on."

"How?" Sex in the past had always been fast, clinical. A drive to scratch an itch. "Tell me."

He wanted to know everything about pleasuring this woman.

"My breasts. They feel full. And my skin is sensitive."

He pulled back a little. "Show me." All thought had fled his head. All he needed was to see her, feel her, and touch her. He sank his fingers into the tiny scrap of emerald silk covering her and yanked it away.

She gasped, her small breasts bared to him. Then he leaned down and sucked one sweet nipple into his mouth.

"Yes. Like that." Her fingers dug into his scalp. "A little harder."

He did as she asked and then moved over to the other nipple. She was the perfect handful, and he loved the way her nipples darkened and pebbled.

"What else?" he murmured against her skin.

"My belly feels tight, like there are a hundred butterflies winging around in there." She sucked in a breath. "I'm damp between my legs."

Drak. His cock leaped against his trousers. He moved downward, peppering kisses across her skin. He pressed a kiss to her belly, letting his tongue delve inside the tiny divot there, and felt her quiver against his mouth. He nipped at her hipbone and she arched into his caress.

He flicked open her trousers, grabbed the slick fabric, and yanked them down her slim legs. She lay naked before him, pale skin, delicate muscles, and more of those maddening freckles.

"I overheard Raiden and Thorin talking."

Her green-gold eyes blinked up at him. "And?"

Kace moved his mouth lower, pressing his lips just above the fascinating tangle of red hair between her legs.

"They were talking about a small bundle of nerves..." Kace slid his hand down, parting her folds. She was so pretty, and pink, and soft.

Another throaty laugh. "Typical men. It's called the clitoris." Her voice turned breathy. "Women here don't have them?"

"I believe they are in a different location." He moved his finger until he brushed a small nub.

When her body jerked and a cry was torn from her lips, he knew he'd found the right spot.

"You…don't know for yourself?" she asked.

"I haven't been with a woman here on Carthago. And Antarian women find pleasure in intercourse."

"Well, some Earth women do, too, but the clit is where most of the action happens."

When Kace rubbed the tiny knot, her breathing turned choppy. "Action?"

"Action…the things you do, when it's good…" She threw her hands out on the mat. "Stimulation, licking, sucking."

Kace went still. "Licking and sucking?" Desire exploded inside him, fire eating at his gut.

"Yes." She lifted her head. "Kace—"

He had to taste her. He leaned down, parted her thighs, and licked her.

"God." She reared up.

He held her down and started sucking on her clit. As she cried out his name, he alternated between licking and sucking.

She was so responsive, and he found it so easy to determine what she liked best. Her hands were back in his hair, tugging hard. His cock was hard and throbbing. The taste of her was so intoxicating.

He smiled against her skin, liking how she was going wild for him. He watched her every reaction, and when something got a strong response, he did it again. And again.

"Kace!"

He felt her body tensing beneath his, and knew her release was coming soon. He moved down, stabbing his tongue inside her, licking at her juices.

And then he moved back up to that small little nub that was so fascinating. He sucked it into his mouth.

And with another arch of her back and a wild cry, Rory came, crying out his name.

***

Rory felt dazed, and so very relaxed. She lay sprawled on the mats, her damp skin cooling, and Kace's head pressed against her belly.

She idly stroked his thick hair, listening to his irregular breathing.

Once she could move, she was going to lay him back, strip him bare, and lick every tough inch of him. He'd just given her one of the best, most mind-blowing orgasms of her life.

She wanted to return the favor.

Rory was just about to move when he pushed off her and stood.

She froze. His body was rigid, closed-off. Surely, he wasn't going to leave her…again?

She forced herself to look up, and dread solidified in her belly. His face looked so torn. She saw desire warring with guilt and torment.

He was going to leave.

Suddenly, Rory felt horribly naked and exposed. She sat up and pulled her legs in to her chest. She wrapped her arms over her bare breasts. "Why?" A single, harsh word.

"Because I'm not allowed to want you. I'm not allowed to put my own needs before my people."

She watched as his hands flexed and curled by his sides.

"Kace—"

"I'm sorry." He turned and hurried out.

Rory slapped the mat. *Damn him.* She was tired of him touching her and then walking away. It hurt. It hurt so damn bad.

She flopped back on the mat, staring at the ceiling. But a part of her felt sorry for him. She could see the torment stamped on his expression, in his eyes. He wanted her, but that apparently went against his beliefs. She was only making this worse for him.

She had the unhappy realization that Kace would never truly be hers. Even if he did pull her into his arms and become her lover, she'd never be able to compete with his sense of duty and honor.

Eventually, he would leave her.

For the first time in her life, Rory found a problem that she couldn't attack or beat up, or solve through any of her usual methods.

Slowly, feeling very old, she pulled herself onto her knees and grabbed her clothes. She dressed and left the gym.

As she walked through the now-silent corridors, her clothing rubbed against the sensitive and still-swollen flesh between her legs. She could still feel his mouth and tongue on her. In her. *God.*

She walked into the living quarters, which were now thankfully quiet. The party was over, or had at least moved somewhere more private.

She was almost to the corridor leading to the bedrooms, when Regan entered the room. Her cousin looked flushed, eyes bright, her white nightgown brushing over her clearly naked body beneath.

"Oh. Rory. I was coming to get a drink. I thought you were in bed already."

"On my way." Rory's belly tightened painfully. Regan had the look of a woman who'd been well loved.

"What's wrong?" Regan frowned at her, and reached out one hand.

"Nothing." Rory evaded her cousin's touch.

"You've got your sad face on." A line appeared on Regan's forehead. "It's the look you usually hide under your 'get out of my way or I'll beat you up' face."

A reluctant smile tugged at Rory's lips. "I can never hide from you. Don't worry, I'm just a little bit sad."

Regan opened her arms and Rory moved in for a hug. As her cousin's slim arms folded around her, Rory leaned into her, absorbing the feel and comfort of her.

"I know it's hard," Regan murmured. "Thinking about everyone at home. And I know how close you are to your family."

Rory hugged her cousin back harder. She felt a shot of guilt for letting Regan think she was sad about home. Then Rory pulled back and straightened her shoulders. If she let herself wallow in her misery, she'd fall down in a pile and not get back up. "You get back to your big, bad gladiator."

Regan hesitated. "You sure? We could—"

"Go." Rory shooed her off. The last thing she wanted was to play third wheel. "I'm off to bed." Alone.

She left Regan to get her drink, and moved into her room, closing the door quietly behind her.

The room was awash in moonlight. Feeling incredibly tired, Rory stripped off her clothes and pulled on a simple sleeping shirt. It hung off one shoulder and fell to mid-thigh.

She wandered over to the window and stared out at the moonlight. She had to remind herself she wasn't alone. Not anymore. Not like Madeline.

Where the hell are you, Madeline? Could the other woman see the moon? Or was she locked up in a windowless cell, alone and hurting?

With a shake of her head, Rory climbed onto the bed.

She lay back against the sheets, and tried not to think of Kace.

Of course, she thought of Kace.

No. No more thinking about the man. She stared up at the ceiling, and willed herself to think of anything except the tough, sexy gladiator who clearly didn't want her.

Then she heard a faint noise... A scuffling sound.

Rory sat up. She stared around the shadow-and-moonlight-filled room. She saw nothing but the shifting shadows, and the gauzy curtains at the windows blowing in a slight breeze.

She was just about to lie back down when a skittering noise on the floor caught her ear.

Slowly, she swung her legs over the edge of the bed and flicked on the light beside the bed. She glanced around and spotted a shadow of something darting under the bed.

Heart thumping, she reached for her toolbox and pulled out the nearest tool. She didn't even look at it, so she wasn't even sure what the alien tool was, but it was heavy and solid. She held it up and walked back toward the bed. She flicked up the covers and looked under the frame.

Nothing.

She circled around the bed. Maybe she'd just been imagining things. It'd been a pretty trying night.

But then she heard another whisper of noise.

She froze, and something burst out from under the bed.

The creature came at her fast. The quick glimpse she got made her think of a spider, with a silver-gray skin.

She dodged to the side and the basketball-sized beast hit the floor, skittering on its legs to find purchase.

No. Not a spider. It was more like a scorpion, a pointed tail rising up with a sharp stinger on the end. The only difference was, it had more legs.

Great, it was a scorpion spider.

She watched the creature dart forward, then slammed the tool down and whacked at it.

Without a sound, the scorpion spider scuttled backward.

Then it shot forward again, aiming at her legs. Seconds later, a sharp, horrible sting burned her left calf.

Ow. Shit.

Rory kicked out, and the creature leaped off the ground, higher than Rory would have thought possible. She dropped the tool, and gripped the beast in her hands, wrestling against it, as it aimed its stinger toward her face.

She shot backward, until her back thudded against the wall, fighting desperately to hold the damn thing off her. She watched in horror, as the stinger shot forward, toward her eyes. She wrenched her neck to the side, and the stinger thumped against the wall. It stabbed again and she jerked her head in the other direction.

Straining, Rory pushed against the creature's surprisingly powerful body. "Screw you, you ugly little fucker. I'm not planning to die today."

Chapter Nine

Kace lay sleeplessly in his bed, and knew there was no way he was going to be able to rest any time soon.

He was very conscious of the fact that Rory was in the room next door. Only one wall separated them.

Desire still burned in his gut. His jaw locked, and he stared at the ceiling. Even the light sheets were too much on his naked body. He shoved them back, then reached down and curled his hand around his rock-hard cock.

He stroked himself, his quiet groan echoing in the room. *Drak*. He was an Antarian soldier, and supposed to have unshakable control.

He squeezed his eyes shut, moving his hand faster, reliving those moments in the gym, Rory's cries of pleasure. The Earth woman was ruining him.

Suddenly, he heard a noise. A thump against the wall between their rooms. Frowning, Kace sat up.

There was another thump, and he strained to hear more, to find the cause. Then he heard something else. The faint sound of Rory cursing.

He jumped up. Something was wrong. He reached out and grabbed his staff from beside the bed where he kept it.

Without stopping to think, he slammed out of his room, and a second later, he shoved open the door to Rory's room.

Drak. She was fighting off a *krath*.

Kace sprinted across the room. She was barely keeping the deadly creature away from her face. Any second now, and the beast's stinger would hit her.

He grabbed the creature by the legs. "Let go."

Her face was flushed with strain. As her gaze locked on his, she nodded and let go.

He gripped the beast, turned, and threw it with all his strength. It hit the far wall with a heavy smack, and dropped to the ground.

By the time the *krath* scrambled back onto its feet, Kace was already there. He lifted his staff and aimed for the deadly thing.

It scuttled to the side, dodging the blow. Then it rushed forward, trying to slip around him and get to Rory.

He knew once a *krath* had a scent, it never gave up.

The creature jumped. It flew over Kace's shoulder, and slammed into Rory.

With a horrified scream, she fell to the floor, wrestling the animal.

"Rory!"

Kace tore the *krath* off her. As she rolled away, he stabbed at the drakking creature with his staff.

This time, he didn't miss.

It let out a near-silent hiss and wobbled, clearly stunned. Kace hit it again, and again. The image of Rory trapped against the wall, holding it off, was burned into his brain. He slammed the staff down again, and this time, the *krath* fell onto its back, its legs twitching.

He hit it a final time and this time it went still.

Rory was huddled on the floor by the bed. She was panting, her hair in disarray, her face flushed. A simple sleep shirt left her legs bare, and made it clear she had nothing on underneath the soft fabric.

"Are you hurt? Did it sting you?" The *krath*'s poison was lethal.

"Fuck." She stared at the carcass. "Nasty little thing." She held one leg out. "It scratched me, but it doesn't hurt now."

He saw the angry red line on her skin, but not the telltale blackening that indicated *krath* poisoning. He strode over to take a closer look, then exhaled, relieved. "It didn't inject its toxin."

She nodded and lifted her head to look at him. Her gaze reached his waist, and her eyes widened.

Drak. He'd forgotten he was naked. Her gaze was locked on his still-hard cock, which was currently right in line with her face.

His stomach tightened. He watched, as Rory licked her lips, and his cock jerked.

Suddenly, the door burst open behind them. The others flooded into the room—Raiden, Harper, Thorin, Saff, Lore, and Nero.

Raiden looked at a near-naked Rory, then his gaze moved to Kace's naked body, then to the carcass of the dead *krath* on the floor.

"What the hell?" Raiden bit out.

Saff was grinning. "Well, military man. Apparently, you really know how to show a girl a good time."

Drakking hell. Kace yanked the sheet off the bed and wrapped it around his hips.

***

Rory sat at the table in the living area, cradling a mug of hot *ocla* that Saff had brought her. Rory was considering how to beg the woman for some of her stash of the stuff. It tasted like coffee blended with hot chocolate.

Exactly what she needed right now.

Regan settled a blanket around Rory's shoulders. "How are you feeling?"

"Better." Her hands were still shaking a little, but she wasn't about to admit that to anyone.

Harper moved up on her other side and squeezed her shoulder.

A second later, Kace strode in. He was wearing trousers now, but no shirt. It didn't matter. She could still see the image of his long, thick cock seared into her brain.

Apparently, some ugly-ass alien creature trying to kill her wasn't enough to stifle her lust for Kace Tameron.

"What the hell was that creature?" Harper demanded.

"It was a *krath* assassin bug," Kace ground out. "Our rivals, the Hemm'Darr use them, but they are common across the main systems."

"Assassin bug?" Rory frowned. "I don't understand. What would it be doing in my room?"

"Could it have come in the window?" Raiden suggested.

Kace's mouth tightened. "They're good climbers, but that's a long way, even for a *krath*."

"So we have a traitor in the House of Galen." Raiden's voice turned Arctic.

"Did someone put it in my room by accident?" Rory still couldn't understand who'd want to kill her.

"This is no mistake." Kace's blue eyes looked dark. "*Krath* are fed the scent of their prey. Someone is definitely trying to kill you."

God. "Why?"

"You know something," he answered.

Rory set her mug down and threw her hands up. "What could I possibly know? I can't think of anything. All I know for certain is that it would take two hundred years to reach my planet, the Thraxians are vicious slavers, and the Vorn are insane. I get the impression that none of this is news to anybody. I don't know anything special about any of them."

Kace knelt in front of her. "Think, Rory."

"I don't know."

His gaze burned into her. "Think, if you want to live."

"Okay, Kace, lay off," Raiden said.

"You're okay." Regan wrapped an arm around Rory's shoulders. "That's the main thing."

"The Thraxians are toying with us."

Rory looked up and saw Galen had soundlessly entered the room at some point. The imperator was dressed in all black, leaning against the wall.

Galen's voice was dark and lethal. "They are taking jabs at us, and it stops now."

"What can we do?" Saff asked.

"I'm tired of being on the defense," Galen said. "It's time to take the offense."

"The biggest blow we can give the Thraxians is getting Madeline Cochran back from them," Kace said. "They're taunting us with her, but they don't want us to find her."

"But we've been searching," Rory said. "So how the hell do we find her?"

"We know they aren't keeping her in the House of Thrax. So, what other locations do they use?" Kace's gaze moved over his fellow gladiators. "Who else are they friends with?"

Looking at him, Rory saw the military commander he was when he wasn't in the arena.

"No one is friends with the Thraxians," Galen added. "But they do have business associates and allies."

Raiden nodded. "They have some small-time scumbag slavers who feed them fresh stock for the arena." He looked at Rory and the others. "These are people who are not part of the houses. They don't have the money, prestige, or skills to run a house."

"The wannabes," Harper said.

"Yes," Raiden said. "They are the bottom-feeders of Carthago."

Galen shifted. "Rory, did you see any particular aliens visit the Thraxians, bringing them slaves?"

Rory frowned. "There were always people coming and going." She forced herself to revisit the memories. Instantly, goose bumps broke out over her skin, and one memory jumped to the forefront. "There were some aliens who visited a lot. They brought in slaves who weren't very healthy." She exhaled loudly. "Those poor slaves were always badly injured. Like they'd already been in the arena."

Kace straightened. "Can you describe the aliens?"

"They weren't pretty. They were average height, around the same size as all of you, and with stocky builds, but they had deformed heads and faces."

"What do you mean?"

"Ugly skin growths and scars. Like they'd suffered burns or some sort of disease."

Kace shot to his feet, muttering under his breath. She saw the other gladiators all stiffen.

"Who are they?" she asked.

Kace scowled. "The Srinar. The underground fight masters."

Rory blinked and looked at Harper. "Underground fight masters?"

Her friend was frowning and gave a shrug. She was watching the gladiators carefully.

"The Srinar were almost decimated by a plague decades ago," Galen said. "The survivors were horribly disfigured, and they torched their entire planet—their cities, farms, dead bodies, everything—to eradicate it."

"With nothing left, they spread out through the systems," Kace said. "They had no honor. They believed their misfortune gave them the right to take from others. They became pirates, smugglers, gang leaders."

"Here on Carthago," Galen continued, "they are scum. The worst of the worst. Many years ago, they were banned from the arena, and from that time onward, they've supplied poor-quality and mistreated slaves to houses like Thrax. On top of that, we believe they run underground fights."

Raiden crossed his arms over his chest. "There have always been rumors of an underground fight ring, located deep below the arena and the city."

"We've tried to find it," Galen added. "But we've never been able to track it down. People who go there are forbidden to speak of it. The few who do have always turned up dead, their bodies beaten to unrecognizable pulp."

"I'm assuming fighting in this underground ring doesn't bring the same kind of money and prestige as the arena," Rory said.

"You would be right," Galen said, "but…"

Rory wondered what would make a man as tough as Galen pause. "But?"

The imperator's face remained impassive but he released a long breath. "They say in the underground arena, the fights are always to the death."

God. Rory went stiff, and she heard Regan gasp. Surely, Madeline wasn't down there.

"All right, we'll follow up on the Srinar in the morning. For now, everyone get some sleep." Galen's gaze swept the room. "Someone needs to watch over Rory—"

"I will." Kace's tone was firm.

No one argued with him. As everyone filed out, Harper and Regan both gave Rory hugs, and Saff patted her gently on the shoulder.

Great. She was already practically an insomniac, and now she had to have the object of her obsession watch her struggle with her nightmares. Just peachy.

Rory walked back to her room, Kace a big, silent shadow behind her.

She paused in the doorway, her pulse spiking as she carefully scanned the shadows and listened for any tell-tale noises.

Kace brushed past her and did a lap of the room. He checked under the bed, under chairs, out on her small balcony. He closed her windows up tight.

"It's clear."

The deep rumble of his voice made her feel a bit better. She sat on the bed, and knew there was no way in hell she'd ever get to sleep. Not with everything that had happened, and certainly not with Kace beside her.

She stared at the wall, torn between feeling miserable and very, very aware.

Kace sighed, and then he sat down beside her, the bed dipping under his larger frame. “You need some rest.”

“I haven’t slept for more than a couple of hours a night since I got here.” She tucked a strand of her hair behind her ear. “I’ve gotten used to running on limited rest.”

He reached out, his knuckles brushing her cheekbone. Her throat went tight, and she felt that light touch all the way to her core.

“Please…” The word came out choked. “Don’t be kind to me. I can’t handle it when I know you’ll just pull away again.”

She saw a muscle tick in his jaw, and his hand dropped away. A part of her mourned the loss of contact.

They both sat there, separated by just a few inches of space that felt more like a few light years.

A second later, he started singing.

Rory looked up at him, her mouth dropping open. His voice was low, deep, and beautiful. She’d never heard a male voice so melodious. She listened, rapt, letting the dulcet tones surround her. The fact that she couldn’t understand the beautiful, flowing alien words didn’t matter.

He paused. “These are ancient incantations of an Antarian soldier. They are sung to us as children, and we learn to recite them in our heads to help us sleep on the battlefield.”

Those words made her sad. She imagined a

small, blue-eyed boy lying in bed, with no loving arms to hold him when he was lonely, sad or sick.

Then he started singing again, and it was so beautiful that it made the sadness disappear. God, she could lie here forever and listen to this man sing.

Slowly, sleepiness washed over her. She felt safe with Kace. There was no need to be on guard, no need to fight, no need to be afraid.

She tipped over and rested her head in his lap. She saw his hand hesitate, and then it came down and stroked her hair.

With Kace's voice in her ears and his hand playing with her hair, Rory drifted off to sleep.

Chapter Ten

"Goddammit!" Rory threw her glass across the room. It hit a couch, rebounded, and landed on a rug, unharmed.

She jumped to her feet and paced across the living area.

She turned, throwing her hands into the air. "I can't even break a glass right!"

Kace stayed where he was, leaning against the wall. She'd been like this all day—full of nervous energy, muttering under her breath.

He couldn't take his eyes off her.

Just like last night, as he'd watched her sleep. He'd felt a deep sense of satisfaction that she'd slept beside him for the rest of the night.

He glanced over at the screen on the wall. It was full of information Zhim had sent through, and Rory had been poring over it all day. But she hadn't discovered anything to help her understand why someone was trying to kill her, where Madeline was, or how to find the underground fight ring. Hence, this most recent outburst.

He'd lost count of her impressive displays of temper. Regan had told him it was a common thought on Earth that people with red hair had wild tempers. So far, Rory wasn't proving that theory wrong.

"You should—"

She rounded on him, her green-gold eyes sparking. "You tell me to recite a chant again, and I'll punch you in the face."

Kace raised a brow. It showed just how far he'd fallen from Antarian Military perfection, that this angry woman threatening him turned him on.

"There's nothing in this data on underground fights or how to find them." She thrust her hands onto her hips.

"It's kept a tightly-held secret," he said. "I told you that you wouldn't find anything."

She made a strangled noise and resumed her pacing.

Kace rubbed his chin thoughtfully. Rory needed to do something to ease the tension, or she was going to implode. "Want to spar in the gym?"

She snorted. "Remember what happened the last time we did that?"

Yes. He did. Every glorious detail.

"I want to find Madeline," she said. "I want to work out why someone wants to kill me."

Kace did, too. But most of all, he just wanted to look after Rory. He'd spent the night in her room, watching her sleep, and listening to her breathe. She wasn't a calm sleeper, tossing, turning, and using every inch of her bed.

If she shared his bed, he'd hold her in place and ensure she got the sleep she needed. He swallowed. He should not be thinking those kinds of thoughts.

He tried to dredge up the Antarian Military Code to go over in his head.

But as he watched Rory's slim legs as she continued her pacing, the Code seemed like a distant dream written in an alien language.

"You need a break," he told her.

"No."

"Yes."

"You aren't the boss of me." Her nose wrinkled. "Oh God, you've got me sounding like a preschooler."

Kace wasn't exactly sure what a preschooler was, but he guessed she wasn't happy about acting like one.

She strode up to him. "Take me to the Kor Magna Markets. I want to ask around and see if anyone's seen Madeline, or knows how to get down to the underground fight ring."

He crossed his arms over his chest. "You what?"

"The Srinar are down below, somewhere. And so are the answers we need."

Kace shook his head. This was a dangerous idea. "The fight ring is hidden, and you'll never find people willing to talk about it. You start asking questions, and someone will come to shut you up."

"Pretty sure the Thraxians are already trying to kill me."

"More reason not to parade around the market." He touched her hair. "This is far too distinctive."

"I'll be careful, and wear a cloak. I'm not stupid, Kace. That's why I'm asking you to come with me."

With her direct gaze on him, pleading with him,

he felt his resolve waver. "No one will talk."

"I'll never know unless I try."

"No." Kace was well-known on Antar for issuing firm orders. Orders that no one ever questioned.

So he was more than a little bemused when half an hour later, he found himself taking the spiral sinkhole ramp down into the Kor Magna Markets with Rory by his side.

The underground network of tunnels opened up before them. It was packed with stalls and people. He picked up the scents of both fresh and cooked food, and heard a jumble of voices—some raised as they hawked their wares. The tunnels were illuminated by light filtering down through other sinkholes, and by orange lamps attached to the carved rock walls.

In the District, the tourists could find everything they wanted—gambling, drugs, sex. In the markets, the locals could find everything they wanted—food, clothing, crafts, weapons.

Kace watched Rory taking it all in. Harper and Raiden stepped up behind them.

"For the record, I still think this is a bad idea," Raiden grumbled.

"You aren't the only one," Kace said.

But Rory talked him into it, and Harper and Raiden had agreed to come to help watch her back while they were down here. Kace had been overpowered once before, and Regan had been snatched. He sure as hell wasn't making the same mistake again.

They moved past the main hub of the market

and its loaded stalls. He noticed Rory eyeing the stalls filled with weapons and tech. But if they were ever to find a way into the underground fight rings, they had to go into the deeper, darker recesses of the market.

Taking a side tunnel, they moved into an area where the walls moved closer, and the shadows grew longer. Here, fewer lanterns gleamed from the rock, and groups of people congregated against the walls, loitering. These people weren't the smiling, more prosperous stall owners and shoppers in the main part of the market. These ones wore ragged clothes, with weapons worn openly, desperation, fear, and suspicion on their lean faces.

Kace didn't like the way some of the men watched Rory. He made eye contact with more than one or two, and after some scowls, they looked away.

Rory walked up to a group of older men and women holding baskets filled with fruit and vegetables. "Hi, my name's Rory, I'm looking for a friend."

A few people were polite, but no one recognized Madeline's description. As soon as Rory mentioned underground fight rings, people clammed up and scuttled off. As they moved into another tunnel, Kace saw the word had traveled. Most people took off before Rory could reach them.

She sighed. "Nothing." She shook her head. "But I can tell people know something."

Kace shared a look with Raiden. Yes, that was his view, too. A few of the people hadn't been quick enough to hide their reactions.

As they moved deeper through the tunnels, Kace kept his attention moving. He noted an old woman watching them from a nearby tunnel entrance. She peered around the edge, staring at Rory. When she noticed Kace watching her, she pulled back and disappeared.

But as they moved into a new set of tunnels, and Harper and Rory stopped to talk to a small crowd of teenage children, he spotted the old lady again.

She was covered in a cloak made of rough, gray fabric, a hood pulled over her head. He could only see the bottom of her wrinkled face, but he also saw scars. Her back was bent in a way that had to be painful.

It took him a second to realize what she was. The woman was a former gladiator.

She would have fought in the arena years ago, and been injured numerous times. Back before the high-tech medical technology that the houses used today to heal and keep gladiators in peak physical condition.

They got closer, and this time the woman didn't scamper away.

The woman moved, her gnarled hands twisting in her cloak. "I've seen your friend." Her voice was barely more than a rusty whisper.

Rory's eyes widened, and she reached out a hand. "What can you tell me—?"

The woman shook her head, pulling her cloak around herself tightly. "Not here. Too many people listening. Come with me."

Rory and Harper followed the woman instantly. Kace and Raiden followed and shared a look. Kace knew the other gladiator was thinking the same thing—this could be a trap.

Kace reached back and touched where his staff protruded above his shoulder. Ready for him to grab when needed. He noted Raiden resting a hand on the hilt of his sword.

They followed the woman down some older, twisting tunnels stained with graffiti. She led them through a narrow doorway.

A large fan rotated in the wall, and the hum of equipment reached Kace's ears. He realized it was some sort of ventilation room that kept air moving through the underground tunnels of the market.

"I can't risk anyone overhearing," the woman said.

"What's your name?" Rory asked.

"Hilea."

Rory reached for the woman's gnarled hand, but hesitated, and didn't make contact. "You've seen our friend, Hilea?"

The old woman nodded. "Yes. Yes, I saw her. Dark hair that finishes here—" Hilea stabbed her palm at her jawline.

Kace saw Rory pull in a shuddering breath. "That's right. Where is she? Where did you see her?"

"Underground—" Suddenly, Hilea's dark eyes went blank. She blinked at all of them, confusion twisting the scars on her face. "Who are you people?"

Kace went still, studying the woman. He saw Rory and Harper trade a puzzled look.

"You brought us here," Rory said slowly. "Hilea, you said you've seen my friend. You were going to tell me about the underground fight rings."

The old woman blinked and blinked again. She pressed a palm to the side of her head, hitting it a couple of times. Kace had seen it before—Hilea had a long-term head injury.

"You asked to talk to us," Rory continued.

Suddenly, the woman's gaze sharpened. "Right. Right. You're looking for your friend."

"My friend. Her name is Madeline and she's small like me," Rory said.

The woman's eyes focused on Rory and Harper. "The Earth woman."

Rory reached out, but the woman pulled back before Rory could touch her.

Kace felt a rush of sympathy. Hilea had been used up and spat out by the arena, and now she was down here, living like a rat.

"The Thraxians call her bait," the woman said. "They want you, the woman with red hair, dead."

Kace sucked in a breath and he saw Rory's jaw tighten. So it was the sand-sucking Thraxians. "Why?"

"You have the Talos."

Talos? Kace frowned. What the hell was the Talos?

"We don't know what the Talos is," Raiden said.

"Can you tell us what it is, Hilea?" Rory asked.

Hilea started blinking. "Who are you people?"

She pressed her palm to her temple.

Rory sighed. “You asked to talk to us. Can you tell me where the underground fight rings are?”

Fear skittered over the woman’s face. “Don’t go there.”

“I have to find my friend.”

The woman shook her head. “Don’t go there. It breaks a person. You can never pick up the pieces. You can never put yourself back together.” Hilea gripped Rory’s arm, her ragged nails digging into Rory’s skin. “Don’t go there.”

Hilea staggered back and opened her palm. On it was a small coin with an image on it. She glanced at them all, then turned and rushed out. The coin fell onto the floor with a metallic tinkle.

Rory bent down and picked it up. “What’s this?”

The coin was a bright copper color, stamped with a stylized lightning bolt.

Kace looked at the coin with a frown. It looked familiar.

“That is not local currency,” Raiden said.

Rory gasped. “It looks like the coin Malix gave me.”

The memory hit Kace. “The sponsor at the party.”

She nodded, stroking the coin. “He said it was an invite to something.”

Raiden frowned at the coin. “We need to find someone who knows what it is. Someone with lots of information.”

Kace grimaced. “Looks like we need to talk to Zhim again.”

Chapter Eleven

Rory's fingers clenched around the coin, the edges biting into her skin. They were back in the main part of the market, heading for the exit. She was feeling edgy and dissatisfied. She'd wanted to find Madeline or at least the location of the underground fight rings.

But Rory reminded herself they had more to go on than they did before.

"Rory, wait." Kace's large hand wrapped around her arm. "Are you okay?" His gaze searched her face.

She drew in a long breath and caught a hint of his scent. It steadied her. It was as strong and sure as he was. "No. But we have something to run with now."

He nodded, then pulled her over to a store near the entrance. Harper and Raiden paused nearby, waiting for them.

"Why are we stopping?" she asked.

"I need to get something."

The storeowner, a tall thin man with graying hair and a patch of scales on his forehead, smiled at them. Kace leaned over and started speaking softly to the man. The long table was loaded with electronics. There were screens, appliances she couldn't identify, and the alien equivalent of tablets and computers.

Interest piqued, she touched a few things. She saw a small, perfectly crafted robot. A child's toy, she guessed.

Rory didn't pay much attention to Kace until she heard him raise his voice a little. "I know you keep them. I want one."

The storeowner's eyes turned considering. "They're expensive, gladiator."

Kace held up a token with the logo of the House of Galen on it. "That isn't a problem."

With a nod, the storeowner rummaged below his table, and then came back up with a medium-sized box. He handed it over to Kace.

"What is it?" Rory asked.

"A gift. You'll have to wait until we get back to open it."

A smile tugged her lips. He'd bought her a gift. She eyed the box, curiosity niggling at her.

Soon, they left the markets and made their way back through the city. Before long, they were walking back into the House of Galen.

"Rory?" Raiden's deep voice rumbled beside her.

She turned to look at the gladiator. "Yes?"

"May I have the coin? I'll talk with Galen, and we'll contact Zhim."

With a nod, she set the coin down in Raiden's large palm. "How long do you think it will take for him to give us anything?"

Raiden touched her shoulder. "With Zhim, you

never know. Have patience."

Patience. *Right.* While she sat here, imagining poor Madeline stuck in some underground fight ring. She thought of poor Hilea, about how broken, and damaged, she was.

"Come on." Kace nudged Rory into the living area. He set the box down on the table. "Go ahead." He nodded his head at it.

"I am well aware that you're just trying to distract me." She carefully flicked open the top of the box.

A small smile touched Kace's lips. "Is it working?"

"Yes." Equally distracting was the man's perfect, handsome face. A yearning spread inside her and she had to remind herself that Kace had other priorities, other duties.

Rory peered inside the box. A small head poked out, and she took a step back, letting out a soft gasp.

The head was made of a smooth black plastic, with glowing gold lights for eyes. It tilted its head to the side as it studied Rory, then it lifted two perfectly formed paws onto the edge of the box.

The thing made a mechanical-sounding chirping noise at her. With a single leap, the creature jumped out of the box onto the table.

No, it wasn't a creature. It was a robot. A mechanical, dog-like animal.

"I see people in the District with them," Kace said. "It is a mechanical pet. I thought you might like one."

Rory watched, astonished, as the small, dog-sized robot walked around, appearing to sniff at the table. She knew the thing wouldn't have a sense of smell, but possibly sensors to detect sensory input. Lights blinked along the dog's side. Its head was black, but its body was made from a sleek, gray metal.

It looked up at her and moved closer, nudging its head against her hand. It wanted to be rubbed.

With a laugh, she obliged, rubbing its head, then running a hand down its sleek body. It made another chirping noise and then leaped off the table. It started to explore the room.

"They are made on a planet called Zayno," Kace said. "They have very advanced technology, including some of the best artificial intelligence."

Rory watched as the dog jumped up on a couch, circled around just like a real pet would, and then sat down like it was going to take a nap.

Kace had bought her a pet, because he knew she was upset. She glanced over at the gladiator, drinking in the hard planes of his face.

"You'll have to think of a name for him," Kace said.

He felt something for her, but he kept holding himself back. She knew he was torn between being the perfect Antarian soldier, and being with her.

There was too much inside her right now. She'd lost everything. She was afraid the Thraxians were going to kill Madeline, and she was deathly afraid that Kace was going to break her heart.

Kace wasn't hers, and he would never be.

The dog lifted his head, looking at her. He let out a whine, as though he could detect her turmoil.

"I can't do this." She shook her head.

Kace cocked his head. His small smile disappeared. "Rory—"

"I can't be around you, Kace. You're being nice to me, and I want you, but I know I'm making you question vows that are important to you. Even so, I want you to grab me, touch me, be with me."

His face was frighteningly blank.

"I…I can't do it." Rory drew herself up. "Thanks for this little guy." She went over and scooped up the mechanical pet, and strode out of the room. She walked into her bedroom, set the dog down on the bed, and slammed the door behind her.

It didn't make her feel any better.

The dog whined softly.

Rory dropped onto the bed beside the adorable creature. "Yes, I know exactly how you feel."

***

"I have Zhim pulling info on the term Talos," Galen said. "I've also sent him images of the coins Rory received from the sponsor and the woman below."

"Anything?" Kace asked.

They were standing in Galen's office. The large arched windows behind his huge desk gave a perfect view of the training arena, and the recruits who were busy training. Kace caught a glimpse of Saff's tall form as she put them through their paces.

He saw a flash of red, and spotted Rory down on the sand, as well. She was standing beside Harper, both of them holding nets.

Just looking at her made his chest tighten.

Galen leaned back in his chair. "Zhim recognized the coin. It is an invitation into the underground fight rings. You need to show it in order to get through the door."

"Okay, but does that help us *find* the door in?"

Galen shook his head.

Drak. "And the term Talos?"

Again, Galen shook his head. "Nothing yet."

Kace dragged in a deep breath.

"How's Rory?" Galen asked.

"She's tough." Yes. She was tough. She was also the most infuriating and fascinating woman he'd ever known. She left him so conflicted. He was drowning in all these unfamiliar emotions. Emotions he didn't usually feel, emotions he could usually control.

"She's training with Harper," Galen said.

Kace nodded. She was surrounded by gladiators, in the heart of the House of Galen. She was safe, and that was all that mattered to Kace.

"We need to find out why the Thraxians want her dead, G." Kace's hands curled into fists. "They—"

Boom.

Both men froze. Kace grabbed the edge of the desk as the walls and floor shook.

What the hell?

Galen shot to his feet, and both of them rushed

to look down into the training arena.

Kace's heart stopped. A fire raged in the center of the arena.

Without a word, Kace and Galen both broke into a sprint. They charged out the door and down the corridor, heading into the training arena.

Seconds later, Kace broke out onto the sand, three steps ahead of Galen. Gladiators and new recruits milled around the arena, confused and disoriented, some with blood running down their faces and chests. A few lay on the ground with terrible injuries, while those still standing helped the wounded.

In an instant, he shoved the thoughts about his fellow House mates away, and focused on the center of the arena. A giant, circular, wall of red and gold flames rose up, more than twice his own height. Harper and Raiden stood near it, their attention on Rory.

Rory was trapped in the center of the flames with her new pet huddled by her side.

Rory. Kace charged forward.

"No, Kace—" Galen yelled behind him.

Kace ignored his imperator and raced toward the wall of flames. As he passed a weapons rack, he snatched up a metallic band. He slammed the band onto his wrist, never losing speed, and with a shake and a thought, the *tarion* energy shield extended in front of him.

He leaped through the wall of flames.

The shield took the brunt of the heat, but he still felt the lick of fire on his skin. A second later, he cleared the flames and rolled across the sand.

He jumped to his feet and grabbed Rory. "Are you hurt?"

She had a dazed look in her eyes, but she was on her feet. One side of her face was covered in burns, but she shook her head. "I can't hear you!" she yelled loudly, tapping her ear.

He pulled her in against his chest, trying not to crush her with the strength of his hold. She was alive, and he wanted to hold her as tight as he could and never let go.

"That damn pet jumped on top of me," she shouted again.

Kace glanced down the mechanical pet. One of its flanks was singed black, and a little dented. Its tongue lolled out.

"Then it has my eternal gratitude," Kace said.

When Rory snuggled into him, her hands gripping him, he pulled her even closer.

"Glad you're here, gladiator."

He was glad she was alive. Through the flames, he could see Galen and Raiden directing others to get water onto the inferno.

"I'm...feeling a little woozy." Her face had turned pale, her freckles standing out starkly on the patches of skin that weren't burned.

Kace stared at the fire again. It would take too long for them to put it out. Rory needed the healers now.

He bent and scooped her into his arms. He held up his wrist and the *tarion* extended again. He let out a sharp whistle to the dog, and then ran. He curled around Rory as he jumped back through the wall of fire.

The others surrounded them in an instant.

"Is she okay?" Harper demanded.

Kace held Rory tight. "She's alive. A little singed."

"I'm fine." With her hearing affected, Rory was still shouting. Her dog wormed through the group and plonked himself down by Rory's feet.

Kace looked at Raiden. "What the hell happened?"

"There was an explosive set under the sand in the center of the arena," Raiden said. "Right beneath the net training area."

"Luckily, I have a temper," Rory said loudly. "I threw a fit when my aim was off. I tossed a second net device on the sand in disgust and it triggered something."

So it was pure luck that she hadn't been killed. Kace's hands began to shake. There was no doubt in his mind that the explosive had been set to kill her.

"She needs the healers," Kace said, keeping his voice as measured as he could. "I'll take care of her." He sent his imperator a hard look. *And protect her.*

Galen nodded. "We'll investigate what happened here." His icy gaze swept the training arena. "If we have a traitor in the House of Galen, they will be found…and dealt with."

"Someone take care of Hero," Rory shouted.

"Who?" Kace frowned down at her.

"My dog."

Kace caught Raiden's gaze and jerked his head to the mechanical pet. Raiden eyed the dented machine impassively and nodded.

Kace strode inside and headed straight for Medical. It was already busy, with others injured in the explosion being brought in.

"I really am okay," Rory said.

He ignored her and set her on the bed. When she tried to sit up, he shot her a hard look. "I'll hold you down if I have to."

She huffed out a breath and dropped back on the pillow.

A tall, slender Hermia healer arrived, with sand-colored robes and a serene face. The genderless race was renowned as some of the best healers in the galaxy, with the ability to manipulate biological energy to heal.

The healer ran a scanner over Rory. "Minor burns and some internal damage to your ears. You were lucky."

The healer grabbed a long, thin device with a glowing end and inserted it into Rory's ears, first one side, then the other.

"How is that?" the healer asked.

Rory tilted her head side to side. "Much better." Her voice was back to normal volume.

The healer applied med gel to Rory's burns. Thankfully, it was the enhanced gel that Regan had created. Kace watched, as Rory's burns disappeared in just a few minutes.

"Someone tried to kill me again," she said

quietly. It wasn't a question.

For a second, the image of Rory sprawled in the sand, lifeless, gone, appeared in Kace's mind.

He scooped her up. "She's coming with me," he told the Hermia healer.

The healer didn't respond, but Kace saw the resigned look on the healer's face. They were used to dealing with demanding gladiators.

Kace strode toward his room. As he passed through the living area, he spotted a pair of workers cleaning.

"Inform the kitchen that I need a plate of food delivered to my room, please."

The workers nodded. "Yes, gladiator."

As soon as he entered his room, he closed and locked the door. He took Rory into the bathroom and sat her on the edge of the tub. He started running water into the large stone bath.

She watched him quietly.

He turned back to her and started to carefully take off her burned clothes.

"I am not delicate," she said.

"I know." He knew just how strong she was. He eased her shirt off her arms.

"You're acting like I'm fragile."

"You were caught in an explosion, Rory. Just let me look after you."

Once she was naked, he forced himself not to look at her the way he wanted to, and helped her into the tub. She made a small moan, and leaned back in the water.

There was a knock at his bedroom door. The

plate of food. He went out and took it, murmuring his thanks. As he started to close the door, a small body wriggled inside.

Kace looked down at the robot dog. It looked back, tongue lolling. “Don’t make me regret buying you.” But he knew this small machine had tried to protect Rory and for that, he was grateful.

He set the food by the bed and returned to Rory, Hero trotting by his side. She had her head resting on the edge of the bath, eyes closed.

“Someone wanted to see you.”

She opened her eyes and smiled at the dog. “Hey there, boy.” Then she sank deeper into the water. “I don’t want him to see me naked.”

“He’s a machine.”

“And I’m pretty sure he has cameras.” Her gaze narrowed on his damaged side. “I need to fix him.”

“For now, I’ll find him a spot to rest.” Kace led the dog out of the bathroom and out onto the small balcony off his room. He gestured to one of the chairs and Hero leaped up on the cushion. He curled into a ball and Kace gave the dog’s head one pat. “Nice work today, Hero.”

Then Kace wasted no time getting back to Rory. He pulled out a cloth. “Lean forward.” He started washing her back. Her skin was unblemished, but in his mind, he imagined it burned, damaged.

“I don’t want you to treat me like I’m going to break,” she said grumpily.

He kept stroking the cloth over her impossibly smooth skin. She was so small, and someone had almost destroyed her.

"How do you want me to treat you?" he murmured.

She looked back over her shoulder, her red hair spilling down her creamy shoulders. "Like a woman."

Chapter Twelve

Rory couldn't drag her eyes off Kace.

He knelt there, so straight and composed. His bathroom was neat and tidy, and the glimpse she'd seen of his bedroom showed no dirty clothes dropped on the floor, no decorations. Her gladiator was so regimented, but she sensed the passion inside him.

They stared at each other and she felt the pulse of the powerful desire between them.

"I want you, Rory." The words were ripped from him.

She licked her lips. "Against your better judgement—"

"No." She saw the muscles in his neck tense. "An Antarian soldier is, above all else, honest. I haven't been honest with you or myself. I want you, Rory. From the first time you punched me in the face."

A hiccupping laugh escaped her. "You really want this?"

He reached out and grabbed her hand. "Yes."

"You're sure?"

"I almost lost you." His fingers tightened on hers.

Rory was shocked to find his hand was shaking.

"You are mine." His smooth voice deepened to a harsh growl. "No one will hurt you. I'll keep you safe. Protected."

She believed every word. And she believed the hot desire she saw burning in his eyes. "Take your clothes off, gladiator." She barely recognized the husky voice as hers.

He stood, and with methodical movements, he stripped himself bare.

Rory just let herself look at him. Her attention was drawn to the corded muscles of his chest. He was all lickable bronze skin, and the very definition of hard strength. Her gaze skated over the broad shoulders, and the solid and veined muscles of his biceps and forearms. All that work with the staff had left him honed to perfection. Her gaze drifted lower, over the chiseled abdomen and the V of muscles leading downward. She swallowed. The long length of his cock rose up, proud and wanting.

Rory stood in the tub, water streaming down her body.

Now it was Kace's turn to let his eyes drift down her body. Rory had never been shy. She knew she didn't have Harper's strong body or Regan's sexy curves, but she was comfortable with her slim, toned shape. When she saw the faint color tinting his cheekbones, she'd never felt sexier.

She didn't see him move, but suddenly, he stepped into the tub and swept her against his hard chest. His mouth came down on hers in a hard, punishing kiss.

Oh, he tasted so good. She let her hands roam

over his strong shoulders, down his flanks. All that beautiful muscle, just a little leaner than most of the other gladiators. All hers.

His mouth fell away from hers, peppering kisses across her nose and cheeks. It took a second to realize he was kissing her freckles. Then his lips drifted down, across her jaw and then down her neck. He bent her backward over his arm, holding her with ease. He was so strong, and he made her feel protected. Rory had never known how much she wanted that, and had actually fought against it all her life. But now, with her life stripped back to the basics, she understood what it was that she really wanted.

His big hand cupped one of her breasts, and she let out a breathy cry. He gently played with her nipple, and she licked her lips. If her gladiator thought they were going to have sweet, slow sex, he was completely wrong.

He boosted her up and his mouth closed over her small breast. *Oh.* She moaned and slid her hands into his hair. She directed his lips to where she wanted his touch. His clever tongue lapped at her nipple.

"Harder, Kace."

He instantly increased the pressure. "These are so pretty." He murmured the words against her skin as he moved to her other breast.

"I'm getting cold," she murmured. A sweet little fib.

He sank down into the water, pulling her forward until she straddled him. She felt the hardness of his thighs, the coiled strength in his body. She shivered. What would it feel like to have all that strength to herself, as he buried himself inside her?

What would it feel like to see pleasure burst across his face and have this controlled man let go, just for her?

"I've never been with a woman like you," he murmured, his blue eyes taking on a faint glow.

"And I've never been with a man like you." She rocked against him, feeling the iron-hard length of him beneath her. "What do you like, Kace Tameron? What turns you on?"

She felt him go still. "I don't know." A frown appeared on his face. "Right now, I know you ignite a desire inside me like I've never known."

Her heart clenched. He'd never explored what he liked in bed. She felt a hot tingle deep in her belly. They were going to have a lot of fun discovering what he liked…together.

"I'm all yours, pretty boy." She held her arms out, her breasts bobbing in front of his face. "Take what you like. Explore."

He made a hungry sound. But instead of grabbing her, he reached over to a small dispenser on the side of the tub. He poured some liquid soap in his hands and then lathered them up. The look in his eyes… Rory's belly contracted in anticipation.

He stroked his hands over her shoulders, down over her breasts. She shimmied against him, feeling the heat inside her growing. When his slippery hands disappeared beneath the water, and she felt him stroke her clit, she gasped.

She grabbed at his shoulders. "Hey, maybe we should slow—"

"You said I could do what I like." He was using his commander tone.

Rory felt like she was riding the sharp, jagged edge of an orgasm. She wasn't ready yet. She wanted this to last a lot longer. "Yes, but maybe a—"

He plunged two fingers inside her. Rory's back bowed, a strangled cry coming from her throat.

"Let go for me, Rory." He pressed his lips to her neck. "Let me see your pleasure."

God. Let go? Rory was the queen of holding on tight. But as Kace kissed her again, his fingers starting a savage rhythm in and out of her body, she realized she didn't have a choice.

Another hard thrust and she exploded. Her cry echoed off the tiles, water splashing onto the floor. Pleasure left her limp and breathless.

Dimly, she was aware of Kace pulling her close, scooping water on her to rinse off the suds. When she opened her eyes, he was holding her securely in his arms, the water cooling around them, and his cock like iron beneath her.

She needed him inside her. She needed to feel her gladiator stretching her. She wanted him to feel the same pleasure she did.

Rory shifted until she felt the thick head of his cock nudge her folds. Kace went still.

She cupped the side of his face. "What's wrong?"

"I've…never had sex in a bath."

Rory smiled. "First time for everything."

His hands clamped down on her hips. "I've never had sex with a woman on top."

She raised a brow. "What, an Antarian soldier always has to be in charge?"

"Yes."

"Well—" Rory lowered herself down, feeling the hard inches of him stretching her. She heard the hiss of Kace's breath. Damn, he was so hard and thick. She used his shoulder for leverage and thrust down until he was lodged completely inside her.

Kace's hips bucked upward and a shout exploded out of him. He thrust up again, lifting Rory up, and went deeper.

"You're so big," she gasped.

"You're so tight." The words were said between gritted teeth.

She felt his body trembling, his muscles straining, like he was holding himself in check. No. She didn't want his control and care right now. She wanted his passion. She wanted to see him let go and give in to the pleasure.

Rory pressed her mouth to the side of his neck, using her inner muscles to squeeze down on his cock. "Your turn to let go, Kace."

"No." His fingers tightened on her skin. "I will not hurt you."

"I'm not going to break." She nipped at his skin, hard. She lifted her hips, dragging his hard cock out of her.

He growled, his body tensing more.

"I'll enjoy every minute of it, gladiator." She felt hot, her stomach tight with anticipation. "Let go. Take me."

His big body trembled. She bit him again.

His control broke. He slammed her down as he thrust upward.

Her mouth opened with a soundless cry, her back arching as she tried to absorb the impact of him. She was so full, and it felt so good.

She realized he'd gone still again. "Don't you dare stop or I'll give you another black eye."

A strangled laugh. It brought a smile to her lips. Something told her Kace had never laughed during sex before.

He started to move, and she did, too. They found a hard, fast rhythm, water sloshing against the side of the tub. He slid in and out of her with powerful movements.

"You are mine, Rory. There will be no one else."

She cried out, feeling her orgasm charging at her. She wanted to believe those words. So desperately.

"If another man touches you, I will end him," Kace growled, his hips hammering upward.

Rory was beyond conscious thought now. As she exploded into ecstasy, it was his name torn from her lips.

And as she heard Kace roar his release and pour himself inside her, she saw his eyes turn an incandescent blue. *Hers.* Her hands clutched at his shoulders for an anchor, and everything felt right for the first time in forever.

***

It wasn't enough.

Kace sat in the cool water with Rory curled against his chest. The only sound in the room was the heavy pants of their breathing.

He wasn't done yet. He wanted more. No, he needed more.

He lifted her, water sluicing off both of them, and strode into his bedroom. He lowered her down onto the sheets, covering her with his body.

"Hmm." She stretched her arms above her head, looking like a sleek, satisfied feline. "That was—"

He shifted and thrust into her.

She cried out, arching up against him. "God, Kace."

"Too soon?" He held himself above her, impatient, needing more.

"Just surprised." She wrapped her arms and legs around him. "A nice one. Men on Earth need longer to get to round two."

He thrust into her again. "I do not want to hear about men of Earth."

"O-kay," she managed.

He started thrusting into her with a slow, intense focus. In the bath, he'd felt wild, out of control. Now, he wanted to feel it every time she clenched, savor every move and noise she made.

Now, he wanted to claim her as his.

It had been a long time since he'd had a woman.

A long time since his last military leave. Soldiers had to be in top form and leave was strictly regulated.

Her leg curled around his hip. “More.”

She was insatiable. He loved it.

He slammed into her, glorying in the feel of her, in her response. She kissed him, her body moving in time with his. He kept up his powerful thrusts, lights starting to flicker in his eyes, his pleasure clamping down hard at the base of his spine.

She took everything he gave her, this small, strong woman who wanted him as much as he wanted her.

Suddenly, she orgasmed, her cry sharp in his ears. He kept her pinned, driving home, a hard edge riding him.

“More.” His word was barely understandable. “Again.”

She cried out again, finding a second release. And that was enough to drive Kace over the edge. He came, hard.

He rolled to the side, pulling her close. He couldn’t seem to draw air into his burning lungs, and he wasn’t sure he could feel his legs.

Finally, he could think through the haze of pleasure. He moved, sprawling on his back, and pulling Rory up on top of him. She nuzzled her face against his neck, her legs falling to either side of him.

She pressed lazy kisses against his chest. “I like how you’re made, soldier.”

He toyed with her hair. All that gorgeous red

hair. "I like your fire. And I don't just mean the color of your hair."

She lifted her head and grinned at him. "My temper?"

"Yes." Rory embraced life, whatever it threw at her. He admired the hell out of that. "Your family must miss you."

When he saw the pain spasm on her face, he was sorry he'd brought it up.

"I'm sure they do. I'm close to them. My parents, my three brothers. I was the youngest, a little spoiled, and I liked getting my own way."

"That, I can believe."

She slapped his chest playfully.

"I don't pretend to understand the bond of family," he said quietly. "But I can understand how much you must miss them."

She nodded, rubbing her cheek against his skin. "It'll take time to fully accept that I'll never see them again." Her chest hitched. "But I've never been one to wallow, and they wouldn't want me to be unhappy."

He nodded. "My squad is like my family. We've trained together from youth, and now we fight together in battle."

"Will they come to fight in the arena as well?"

He shook his head. "The Antarian military sends soldiers to a lot of different planets to co-op with other fighters and learn new skills. The others in my squad have gone to other planets."

She brushed her fingers across his cheek, then his lips. "And are the others in your squad like you?

Brave heroes?"

"Yes. They give up everything to fight for our planet."

"Are they sexy like you, pretty boy?"

His gaze narrowed. "I am not pretty. And you do not need to concern yourself with their sexiness."

She winked at him, scooting downward. "So, you got to be on top last time, that means it is my turn again."

Kace felt a shot of heat to his system. He imagined her above him, riding him hard.

"I have lots of other positions I want to try as well," she continued.

His gut clenched. "Other positions?"

She nipped his hipbone. "Oh, yes. *Lots* of them."

Kace was trying to imagine these other positions. "I want to try every one." Then her hand closed around his cock.

He sucked in a harsh breath. His gaze was glued to her as she slithered down his body. She pushed her hair to one side so he had a clear view of her face. A clear view as she leaned down and licked the swollen head of his cock.

Even though he'd just had her, his cock filled instantly, growing under her hands. Her eyes widened and she licked her lips.

"Ready to try something else, pretty boy?"

He sank a hand into her hair. "Yes."

He watched as she sucked his cock into her mouth. *Drak.*

Chapter Thirteen

Rory pressed her palms against the stone tiles in the shower. Kace was powering into her from behind, his hands clenching on her hips.

"I like—" he thrust again "—this position."

"Me…too," she gasped.

Rory closed her eyes, savoring every sensation—the hard steel of him, the musky scent of sex, the warm fall of water, and the incredible pleasure cascading through her.

Throughout the afternoon, Kace had proven rather imaginative. When her straight-as-an-arrow gladiator let loose, he could be very creative. And thorough. She was certain there wasn't an inch of her he hadn't explored with his hands, tongue, or cock.

Moaning, she rocked back against him. "More."

This time, he didn't hesitate. He picked up the pace, rocking into her harder than before.

Rory heard hungry little sounds echoing around them, realized they were coming from her. He leaned over her, his chest pressed to her back.

"Come for me, Rory. Now."

Her skin flushed hot, and on his next plunge,

she imploded. A second later, he gripped her hip, thrust deep, and held himself lodged to the hilt as he came.

When they could finally move, they left the shower, and took their time drying each other off. Rory liked seeing the faint smile on Kace's face, and the playful way he wiped the water off her skin.

She wanted to see him like this more often.

They stepped back into the bedroom to find Hero waiting for them, tail wagging. With a smile, she crouched down to pat him. "Hey, boy." She studied his damage again. She had to find some time to fix him.

A hard knock sounded at the door.

"We have a message from Zhim." Galen's clipped voice.

Her throat tightened, and she saw Kace's expression revert to serious soldier. Sighing, she quickly dressed in some fresh clothes a worker had dropped off earlier. *Thank you, Regan.* Rory was going to make sure the scorched clothing was properly disposed of.

When they entered the living area, the others were huddled around the screen dominated by Zhim's striking face. She saw Regan and Harper look her way. Her cousin eyed her and grinned, while Harper looked at Kace, then back at Rory, and winked.

"Intriguing little Rory," Zhim drawled. "How are you today?"

Kace wrapped an arm around her and tugged

her to his side. Rory rolled her eyes. "You want to go ahead and just brand me, pretty boy?"

A few chuckles rolled through the room.

"Perhaps," Kace said.

Zhim's eyes widened. "Oh. Fascinating. I would never have picked an uptight, rigid Antarian for you."

Kace growled, and Rory could almost see the information merchant filing Kace's possessiveness away in a mental data file. "Enough. You have something interesting to tell us?"

"I just got a tip." The man's face turned serious. "Several Srinar have been spotted in the lower bowels of the market. I have it on good authority that where they've congregated is a possible entrance to their underground fight rings."

Rory grabbed Kace's hand. He squeezed her fingers. *This was it.* The chance to find out once and for all why the Thraxians were trying to kill her, and to get Madeline back.

Galen gave a single nod. "Thank you, Zhim." The screen went blank, and Galen looked around the room. "Let's go."

All the gladiators stood.

"We'll need to keep a low profile," Harper said.

Raiden moved forward. "You should stay here, with Rory and Regan."

Rory bristled. "I am not staying here." She stared down the tattooed gladiator. "I will not hide behind you all, let you risk yourselves. This is my life."

When she felt Kace step closer, she was ready

for him to agree with Raiden. She whirled to face him.

"Rory deserves to be a part of this," Kace said.

She opened her mouth, then closed it. She saw the glint of amusement in his gaze. "Thank you."

Raiden sighed. "Fine. But you understand you'll be in danger."

"I'm in danger anyway. I almost died right here in the House of Galen." When she heard Kace make a noise, she regretted having to remind him.

"The perpetrator was caught," Galen said darkly.

Kace's head whipped around. "What? Who? Why wasn't I told?"

Galen raised a dark brow. "You were…busy."

Rory felt an inappropriate laugh bubble up her throat.

"He was a house worker with a secret gambling problem, and a large debt to someone in the District," Galen added. "He's been dealt with."

"I still want to see him," Kace said darkly.

The imperator shot him an icy look. "I can assure you, nothing that you can do to him would be worse than my wrath."

God, the man was scary. Rory swallowed and pressed a hand to Kace's chest. "We have more important things to worry about. Like the people who paid this man."

A muscle ticked in Kace's jaw, but finally, he gave a jerky nod.

Soon, they were all gathered and ready to go. Rory was wearing black leather trousers, and a simple black shirt. She'd never seen all the gladiators so covered up and almost nondescript. Wearing understated black, Saff still looked extraordinary. No one would call her beautiful, but she was striking. Even with only a few of his tattoos peeking out from his sleeves, Raiden's presence was commanding. Thorin radiated wild energy, Lore's sexy smile couldn't be ignored, and Nero's scowl would intimidate anyone, no matter what he was wearing.

Even dressed in their all-black clothes, it didn't quite mask their extraordinary physiques. She looked at Kace's handsome face. These big, tough gladiators would never just blend into the background.

She felt something butt against her feet and looked down at Hero. "You need to stay here, little guy." The dog whined.

"Here." Kace held out a staff to Rory.

Her staff. She gripped it, her fingers closing over the Antarian inscriptions. "Thank you." She swung it around on her back.

Regan came over to Rory. "I'm staying here. Find her, okay?"

Rory hugged her cousin tightly. "We will."

"No one deserves to be helpless and alone."

Rory hugged her harder. They'd all been there, but thanks to these tough gladiators surrounding them, they had the chance for something else, something far better. "Regan, will you take care of Hero for me?"

Her cousin's gaze fell to the dog and she smiled.

"Sure thing." When she opened her arms, the mechanical pet gladly leaped into them.

The group moved fast. Night was falling, and Rory could just make out the stars in the sky blinking into view over the bright lights of the District in the distance. They descended into the Kor Magna Markets and Rory blinked.

She'd expected the place to be winding down for the day. She couldn't have been more wrong.

There were even more people packed into the underground space. Somewhere, music was playing—cheerful tunes of strings and drums. The scents of cooking filled the air—not all of them delicious to her untutored Earth nose—and more lights were on, casting a bright, cheerful glow across the stalls.

Her group moved through the crowd quickly, ignoring the sights and sounds, and soon were heading down darker tunnels. Here, there was no music or bright lights.

"The area where the Srinar were spotted is down a few levels." Galen led them down a ramp.

A number of shady characters were hanging around, interspersed with kids in ragged clothes, and older people sitting on battered stools, and Rory noticed their group was being carefully watched. She scanned the shadows, hoping to see Hilea, but there was no sign of the woman.

Soon, they reached an empty tunnel that finished at a dead end, with a single metal door. This far underground, Rory could no longer hear any sounds from the markets.

Galen nodded to Thorin, and the big gladiator moved forward. With a shove of his large shoulder, the door burst open.

They moved into a large room. It had a vaulted ceiling, and the place was filled with car-sized pieces of equipment. Most of the machines hummed loudly, and a few made clanking sounds. Rory moved closer, her interest piqued. They looked like generators. She followed the black cables running from the appliances up to the ceiling. She started to make her way around the closest machine, and felt something sticky under her feet. Some sort of black substance was leaking from the closest generator. The stuff was dark and viscous like oil.

"These power units provide power to the markets, and to the houses of the people who live down here," Raiden said.

At any other time, Rory would have been interested in studying the technology. She felt that familiar itch to pull something apart and see what made it tick.

But that wasn't why they were here.

They kept moving, and eventually reached the back of the large room. She saw some stacks of old and rusty equipment, and some large wooden crates.

There were no doorways or stairwells leading to secret underground fight rings.

She resisted the urge to kick something. "There's nothing here."

The gladiators spread out, looking around. Kace's face was impassive, but she could tell he was frustrated. He was controlled, but after studying him so much, she'd learned to read the tiny signs he gave off.

Suddenly, as one, the gladiators stiffened and moved back toward her.

She glanced at Harper, who was holding her swords at the ready. Her friend shrugged, her gaze watchful.

"What's wrong?" Rory looked around, a bad feeling growing in her belly.

"I smell Thraxians," Thorin growled, lifting his axe.

Raiden nodded, drawing his sword. "I can sense a foul essence."

Suddenly, the walls shimmered. Huge demonic-looking Thraxians pulled away from the walls, hidden by some sort of camouflage technology.

Shouts filled the space.

"Get back!" Kace shoved Rory backward, toward Harper. Her friend lifted her swords and the two of them moved back toward a large generator. The House of Galen gladiators rushed forward.

Swords smashed against swords. Axes hit staffs.

This wasn't like a fight in the arena. As Kace wielded his staff and the others swung their weapons, she saw that this fight wasn't fancy or flashy. This was hard, economical fighting. And Kace was good at it.

She watched him take down two Thraxians in swift succession, the huge, horned aliens falling to the floor. Beside him, Saff covered another Thraxian in a net, and slid her sword into the alien's shoulder. He slumped back onto the floor with a shout.

And that's when Rory saw a hole open up in the floor. The Thraxian screamed as he fell into the black space, and then the stone closed back up behind him.

"Watch out!" she screamed.

Kace heard her, and turned. He spotted a hole as it opened up right under his feet. He leaped out of the way, just in time.

But more trapdoors were opening. As she and Harper moved closer to the generator, Rory saw one hole open up close by. She glanced down. She wasn't exactly sure what their purpose was, but they looked like they were part of some sort of drainage system.

"Edge to the left," Harper said. Her gaze remained locked straight ahead, watching as Raiden fought viciously with a large Thraxian.

Nearby, Thorin let out a roar and slammed his axe at an opponent. It sliced into the Thraxian's shoulder and hit the wall, rock splintering.

Suddenly, an alien charged at Harper and Rory, his eyes glowing a deranged orange-gold.

Rory lifted her staff, ready to fight. Harper leaped forward, her swords whirling. They hit the Thraxian's axe, and the two of them spun away in a lethal dance. The Thraxian towered over Harper, but her friend's face was hard and set, her skill with the swords obvious, as she battled the alien.

The Thraxian slammed a powerful blow against Harper's sword and Harper cried out, struggling to block the hit. Rory took another step away from the generator, waiting for the chance to jump in and help her friend.

The floor opened up beneath her.

Oh, God.

She fell straight downward and screamed.

***

Kace heard Rory scream.

He spun, and saw her slipping down a trapdoor.

No! He didn't hesitate. He ran the few steps to the hole, leaped into the air, and followed her into the darkness, feet-first.

He hit slick metal and slid downward. He strained to hear Rory, but all he heard was the sound of his leathers on metal. He gathered speed, and braced himself for whatever was coming.

A second later, he saw a flash of light at the bottom. The chute flattened out, and then he shot out the end of it.

He landed in a crouch, and took a second to orient himself.

He was in a small room. Through the doorway beyond, he heard the throb of loud music and the noisy cheer of a crowd.

And straight ahead, Rory was struggling with a large Thraxian.

Kace leaped forward. He swung his staff around and slammed it into the Thraxian's lower back. It was a weak point on the aliens. The Thraxian roared, throwing his head back and releasing Rory.

Spinning, Kace swung his weapon. He smacked it into the Thraxian's side, abdomen, chest. The alien grunted with each blow. Another hit, and the Thraxian went down on one knee.

He raised his head, the tusks beside his mouth stark white against his rough, dark skin. The veins under his skin glowed a virulent orange, and he made an enraged hissing sound.

Kace brought his staff down on the creature's shoulders, then in a sharp side move, hit the back of the alien's head.

His body went lax instantly. Without a sound, he fell to the floor.

Kace grabbed Rory. She had one arm wrapped around her body and was looking around the room, studying the contained pond of black sludge in the corner.

"It's some kind of drainage room," she murmured.

He didn't give a drak what it was. "We need to get out of here."

Rory nodded, casting the unconscious Thraxian one last look. "I want to kick him, but that wouldn't be honorable."

"I won't tell anyone." He wanted to do far worse to the drakking alien. To all of them.

With a small smile, she pressed her hands to Kace's chest. "Thanks for coming after me."

"Always."

"My hero."

He grabbed her hand. "Come on. We need to find a way out." He pulled her to the doorway.

They slipped out of the room, and both of them paused. On this side of the door lay a huge, cavernous space, with roughly-hewn stone walls. It was crowded with aliens of all shapes and sizes. Mostly humanoid, but a large number of others as well. Bodies pressed close, packed in together, as lights strobed across the room. The noise in the room echoed in the huge space.

No one was paying Kace and Rory any attention, and the music was deafeningly loud.

Kace tucked his staff beside him, and gestured for Rory to do the same. He guessed they should stay as inconspicuous as possible. As he scanned the crowd, he noted that most of them were armed in some way.

They moved through the press of people, Kace careful to keep Rory close. They passed a couple pressed against a pole. The man's hands were clamped on the woman's ass as they devoured each other. Right next to them, he saw a reptilian alien swapping coins and tokens with people—clearly gamblers placing their bets. Nearby, a small group of aliens were puffing on long pipes, a cloud of purplish, sweet-smelling smoke hovering over them. Kace wrinkled his nose. He hated the cloying scent of taint—a highly addictive drug.

It was then he spotted something over the heads of the wall of people in front of them.

Cages.

They'd found the underground fight rings.

Alongside the cages, people were bouncing up and down, screaming and cheering, egging on the combatants inside.

"Kill him!"

"Break his neck!"

"Blood! Let's see the blood."

Kace leaned his head closer to Rory, pressing his lips to her ears. "Stay close. We'll take a look around, and then search for a way out." He knew Galen, Raiden, and the others would be searching for them.

Rory nodded. "So this is it? The underground fight rings." She looked up at him. "We need to find Madeline. I'm not leaving until we do."

Drak. He'd been afraid she was going to say that. "We'll look."

What he didn't tell her was that he'd carry her out of here over his shoulder, if he had to. He'd do whatever he had to do to keep her safe.

They passed close to what had to be the main entrance into the underground fight ring. Large Srinar guards flanked the entrance and anyone entering was flashing coins to gain admittance.

The guards were armed. Kace's jaw tightened. They wouldn't be heading out that way.

Pulling Rory under his arm, he scanned ahead, alert for anything. Strobe lights crossed the crowd.

Then he saw a disturbance. A group of Thraxians searching the crowd, coming from the direction of the drainage room where they'd entered from.

Drak. Quickly, he yanked Rory to him. She let out a small *oof.*

"Thraxians," he whispered. He dropped onto the

edge of a couch, ignoring the blissed-out *taint* smokers. He yanked her into his lap, curled his hands into her buttocks, and pressed his mouth to hers.

Chapter Fourteen

Rory moaned against Kace's lips, moving her hips against him.

She knew this was just for show, but damn, the man tasted so good. She kept kissing him, sinking her hands into his hair.

When his lips traveled down her neck, she arched her head back. "Are they almost gone?"

He nipped her skin. "They passed by a few minutes ago."

With a groan, she pulled back. "Then we should get moving."

He urged her hips against him again, and she felt the hard bulge of his erection.

"I know." He groaned. "But you tempt me beyond reason." Finally, he set her on her feet. "We need to keep looking around."

As they moved deeper into the crowd, Rory decided she hated this place. There was an edge—a dark, nasty one. Here, you could feel the hungry desperation of the crowd. It wasn't like the arena spectators above, out to watch something primal, something that connected them to their emotions.

Here, it was about drowning yourself in the

dark, in the vice of your choice, in the misery of others.

Moving closer to one of the cages, Rory heard the brutal blows of flesh striking against flesh.

Steeling herself, she looked at the metal-mesh structure rising above the crowd, lit by blinding spotlights. Scores of spectators stood pressed against the metal, fingers curled into mesh, shouting encouragement or derision at the fighters.

A body slammed into the side, vibrating the metal, and she fought to control her flinch. The giant, red-skinned alien was big and brutal, and covered head to toe in black tattoos.

Across from him, bouncing on his toes, was his opponent. He was a tall humanoid, with pale skin that glowed like moonlight. Blood and sweat streaked his chest. This one was smaller and thinner, but appeared much faster than the tattooed alien.

The men charged at each other again, each raining blows on the other.

This place was horrible. Rory had been to lots of MMA fights. She'd always enjoyed watching the fights, the test of skills.

This was nothing like those fights. This was just brutal.

As she got closer to the cage, she felt the primal excitement pumping off the crowd around them. She was grateful for Kace's steady presence at her back. People were screaming, and everywhere she looked, she saw money exchanging hands.

"The fighters are extra motivated tonight," someone shouted from Rory's left.

"Drak, yeah," another man answered. "Don't blame them. The prize is so small, and little, and delicious. I'd give anything for a female like that."

As the fighters slammed into the cage wall again, the cheering rose to deafening levels.

Rory pressed into Kace, going up on her toes. He leaned down, his warm breath brushing her cheek. "I heard them say a small woman is the prize," she yelled.

Kace's face hardened. "Scum."

Inside the cage, the slim man slammed into the mesh nearby. Rory looked up. His face was right near her. Agony filled his face, terror in his eyes. Their eyes met for a second.

Then his opponent grabbed him, pulled him around, and tossed him to the other side of the cage. The slim man went down on one knee.

The red, tattooed alien raised his arms above his head in a gesture of victory. "I'm going to win! I am Randor!"

Rory sidled closer to one of the spectators beside her. "What's this prize everyone's talking about?" She kept her voice friendly, and a little breathless.

The alien's skin was a deep shade of green, and he towered over her. He didn't take his gaze off the fight, just nodded his head toward the other cages. "She's a pretty thing. Tiny with dark hair." Finally, the green alien looked down at her, his gaze warming. "Almost as pretty as you, sweetheart."

Rory bared her teeth. "I'm not sweet. I bite." She

jerked a thumb behind her. "Just ask him."

The alien chortled, glanced at Kace, and choked on his laugh. Kace slid an arm around her, pulling her back toward him.

Holding onto Kace's arm, Rory led them in the direction the alien had nodded. "The woman sounds like Madeline, Kace. They're offering her as a goddammed prize."

There were four more cages, each containing another deadly fight. Unlike the crowds that sat in the arena above, this crowd was much rougher, more bloodthirsty. Alcohol and drugs flowed freely, and people were having sex around the perimeter. Unknown fluids of every description stained the sticky concrete floor. Rory's nostrils were clogged with the scent of blood, urine, and sweat.

They pushed through the crowd, and she stayed close to Kace, as people parted for his big body. Ahead, another crowd bunched around one of the large support columns that speared upward, to the roof of the cavern.

As they pushed their way through the throng, Rory spotted a small figure chained to the column.

She choked back a cry. Madeline Cochran was chained to the support, her head dangling forward. She was wearing a tiny scrap of a dress the same shade as her dark hair.

Just beyond her was a sunken pit. It was larger than the cages, and circled by some tiered seating. Almost a mini-arena. The seats were crowded, the spectators cheering on the fighters below.

"Let's try and get closer to her," Rory suggested.

Kace scowled. "We should wait for Raiden and the others—"

"We might not have that time. What if someone wins her?"

Kace nodded, and they circled the large, sunken pit. The crowd booed, and from below, the sounds of flesh striking flesh and animalistic grunts reached their ears.

Then the crowd roared its pleasure.

As they made their way slowly around the pit, they passed a railing, and Rory glanced down at the combatants.

Everything inside her froze. *No. It can't be.*

"Rory?" Kace's voice at her ear.

She shoved an alien out of her way, and pressed against the railing. She felt Kace right behind her, staying close and shoving another onlooker away.

Rory stared down into the fighting pit at a darker-skinned, sweat-soaked fighter. A *human* fighter. His skin gleamed under the lights, and his dark hair was plastered against his head. He was staring at the hard-packed ground, his chest heaving, as his dead opponent was dragged off.

Lieutenant Blaine Strong, space marine, from Fortuna Space Station.

"Rory? What's going on?" Kace demanded.

"The fighter. He's from Earth, from my space station."

Kace cursed.

A new fighter stepped into the ring. Blaine didn't move, with the exception of his hands curling into fists.

Blaine's opponent was over seven feet tall, with scaly, blue skin.

"We can't help him right now," Kace said quietly. "There are guards all around the ring. They won't let a fighter just walk out of there."

Rory's gut rolled. Madeline urgently needed her, but walking away from Blaine, leaving him stuck here alone, cut her to shreds. She didn't know him well, but she knew Harper did. What she did know, was that he was a good man and an excellent marine.

He shouldn't be fighting for his life in this dirty fight ring.

"I'm not going to leave you here, Blaine," she murmured the words as a promise to him and to herself, too soft for anyone else to hear.

Kace gripped her hand. "We'll come back for him."

Damn straight. It was a promise.

At that moment, Blaine looked up. His dark gaze hit Rory's and widened in shock.

She raised a hand and mouthed the words. "I'm coming back for you."

Blaine stared at her, something flaring in his dark eyes. The big scaled fighter let out a roar, and started across the pit toward Blaine.

Blaine didn't move, just kept his gaze on Rory. Then he moved his head, the tiniest inclination that no one else would pick up but her.

Then he turned to face the fighter.

As Blaine ducked a swing and landed a hard blow to the alien's midsection, Rory forced herself to turn away. She wanted to rage and hit someone. She wanted to see blood spill on the sand.

She was so tired of not being able to save everybody.

Determination tensed her muscles. But right now, right at this moment, she was sure as hell going to get Madeline out of here.

They moved the last few meters through the crowd toward the pole. The crowd shifted, and Rory jerked upright. "Oh, God. Madeline's gone."

The column was empty.

Kace turned his head, scanning the room. "They've moved her."

Rory's gaze flew over the crowd, her heart thumping, until she spotted a small, dark-haired form. "Over there." She pointed. Through a part in the masses, she saw Madeline being yanked through a doorway by two Srinar aliens.

"It's the winner's room," Kace said. "Once a winner is declared, they'll bring them in there to claim their prize."

Rory's mouth firmed. "Not if we can get her out of there first."

Kace grabbed her shoulder. "We must use caution. We can't go charging in there. It could be full of Srinar and Thraxians."

She gave him a frustrated nod. They neared the door. "No guards."

"It seems they doubt anyone would be crazy enough to steal the prize and try to escape."

At the door, Kace pushed her up against the wall, making it look like they were busy mauling each other. Rory slid her leg up, hooking it over his hip.

They both peeked through the doorway.

"Only the two Srinar," Kace said.

Adrenaline flashed through Rory's veins. She looked up at her handsome hero, the man who'd captured her heart.

He pulled his staff around. "Let's get your friend."

"Thank you, Kace."

He touched her cheek. "Thanks are not necessary. Besides, we are not safe yet."

Rory stealthily pulled her own staff around. They looked at each other, then they rushed into the room together.

Kace slammed his weapon into the closest Srinar. Rory rushed past him and swung her staff at the second Srinar's knees. He fell with a loud cry. She hit him again, swinging upward and catching his chin.

He flew backward and slumped to the ground. Nearby, Kace's Srinar was curled in a ball, out cold.

Rory hurried over to Madeline. She was slumped on the couch, and hadn't moved. "Madeline." Rory touched her pale cheek. The woman's skin was chilled, her eyes glazed. "She's been drugged."

Then the sound of an opening door, and Kace's curse, made Rory spin.

There was a door on the side wall that they hadn't noticed when they'd entered. It had just opened. Ice slid into Rory's veins.

A large group of Srinar and Thraxians stepped

into the room, gazes trained on them.

***

Kace changed his grip on his staff, assessing his options.

There weren't any good ones. They were heavily outnumbered. He stepped in front of the women and lifted his staff.

The crowd parted, the Srinar scuttling backward. A Thraxian with an orange sash across his chest stepped forward. Kace's jaw tightened. The Imperator of the House of Thrax.

"Antarian." The imperator tilted his head. "In service to the arena for training. You are only on Carthago temporarily, surely you have no personal concerns here. You may leave."

Kace didn't move. "Leave?"

"Yes. Leave the women behind, and you can go."

Beside him, he sensed Rory stiffen.

"Just like that?" Kace said. "I can go."

"I have no quarrel with you. I know you Antarians only care for your duty in fighting the Hemm'Darr." The imperator lifted one broad shoulder. "Surely two small, odd women from a nowhere world hardly matter to you."

Kace felt a lick of hot anger threatening his control. Rory was everything—feisty, courageous, spirited. And she was his. He would give his life to protect her.

The Imperator of the House of Thrax had no idea what he was talking about. Rory had forced

Kace to awaken from a deep, frozen sleep. Being with her had made him realize what really mattered.

He looked over at her. She was watching him steadily, with her green-gold eyes.

He arched a brow at her. "What do you think, small, odd woman from Earth?" He saw a shudder run through her. Had she really believed that he'd leave her?

The corner of her mouth tipped up, and she gently patted Madeline's arm. She straightened and shot the imperator a nasty look. "I suggest we kick some Thraxian-Srinar ass."

Kace exploded forward, and Rory moved in the same instant.

As his staff crashed against the sword of a Thraxian, he saw Rory sweep a Srinar off his feet with a swipe of her leg. She followed him down, slamming his head into the floor.

Kace swung his staff, knocking a sword to the ground and swinging his staff into his enemy. He spun, lunged, and took down a Srinar. *Hit. Spin. Strike.* He lifted a boot and kicked another incoming Thraxian in the chest. The alien shouted as he knocked into two of his fellow species, taking them all down.

Rory stepped up beside him, her staff up. Together, they fought through the wall of fighters.

But more and more kept coming. He could see Rory was tiring, and a second later, her staff clattered to the floor.

But she kept fighting, using her deadly hands and feet.

Kace spun again, but this time, a hard blow hit his side. He stumbled, and felt the slash of a sword against his shoulder. He gritted his teeth against the pain, ignoring the slide of blood down his chest.

He saw two Srinar grab Rory, pinning her to the ground.

"No!" He spun his staff, slamming past a Thraxian fighter.

Rory was cursing fiercely and struggling. Kace knocked a Srinar out of the way, then stumbled to a halt.

The Thraxian imperator had yanked her off the floor, and was holding her squirming body against him, a dagger to her throat.

"I need her dead." The imperator shook his head. "You should've taken my offer, Antarian." He looked at his remaining men. "Kill him."

Five Thraxians rushed in. Kace fought hard, but there were too many of them. He absorbed the blows, and took two more down. Then he felt a blade slide between his ribs.

He grunted, but kept fighting.

"No!" Rory's scream.

Movements slowing, blood coating his chest, he swung at another alien. He wouldn't give up, not while there was still breath in his body.

He had to save Rory.

***

Rory had never been more afraid.

The Thraxian imperator held her in a hard grip, his claws digging into her skin. The blade was cutting into her skin and she felt a trickle of blood down her neck.

Her lungs were tight. It was nothing compared to the blood pouring down Kace's chest. Even though his shirt was black, she could see it was soaked. He was fighting, still spinning that wicked staff. But he was slowing down, and his fingers were sticky with blood.

For every alien he took down, another stepped forward to fight him.

She swallowed a sob and then watched, as Kace fell heavily to his knees. His head hung forward, sweat dripping from his hair.

The Thraxians and Srinar circled him. Rory lost sight of him as they started to kick and hit him.

Get back up. "Damn you, get back up, pretty boy." She willed him to rise, as though her thoughts would give him more energy.

Then, a Thraxian went flying into the wall. She saw Kace back on his feet. He was swinging his fists wildly, his moves uncoordinated.

Rory felt as though her chest had turned to stone. He was really hurt. She watched him go down again, a vicious blow that snapped his head back. She wanted to close her eyes, pretend it wasn't happening, but she didn't. They were in this together. She could see the swelling and bruising marring his face and her heart hurt.

He was her hero. Fighting for her to the end.

"Why?" She turned her head and shouted at the imperator. "Why do this? Why do you want to kill me? You said it before, I'm nobody from a nowhere planet."

The Thraxian dragged her around the room, but kept his gaze on Kace. "Because of the Talos."

"What the hell is this damn Talos?"

His claw tapped her neck. "It is an implant. You and the other woman were implanted with them when you came to the House of Thrax."

Her brow wrinkled. "The translator implant?"

He shook his head. "No. Another implant hidden below the translator implant. The Talos is experimental. It is supposed to control our slaves, make them more pliable and biddable. Controllable."

Kace coughed, then his voice rose. "It is against the rules of all the houses." Rory turned and saw Kace on his knees, his face swollen. One blue eye looked straight at them.

The imperator growled. "I will not hear about rules from one of the House of Galen. You break them to steal gladiators from other houses all the time."

"You say steal, we say rescue. There are few rules in the arena, but one is followed by all and has been since the first stone of the Kor Magna Arena was laid," Kace continued. "No technology to enhance or control a gladiator. You have broken that cardinal rule."

The Thraxian imperator lifted his chin, his veins glowing orange. "Don't worry, Antarian. The Talos failed. We are not using them now."

"Naare. The Varinid gladiator who is close to earning his freedom." An expression of understanding softened Kace's hard expression. "He has the implant."

Rory saw something cross the imperator's face, but it was hard to read.

"Yes. But Naare's implant was faulty. He was an early test case, and it destroyed his brain. Like I said, we are no longer risking our investments by using it."

"You haven't been controlling me." Rory felt sick and horrified at the thought that her body had been violated, this implant inside her without her knowledge.

"No. For some reason, the implant failed to affect you and the woman." The imperator cast a glance at Madeline. "Now, I can't afford for anyone to discover the implants. If the other houses knew…no, I cannot have that."

"You mean you're afraid of Galen. He would dismantle your house piece by piece."

"I am not afraid of Galen," the Thraxian spat. "But no one needs to know about the Talos."

Dread settled in Rory's gut. Now that Kace and Rory knew the truth, the odds that they'd get out of this hellhole alive had dropped to zero.

"Finish him," the imperator ordered.

The attack on Kace doubled. Each vicious blow made Rory flinch. When Kace fell down onto his hands and knees, struggling to get back up, she couldn't take it anymore.

She thrust an elbow back into the imperator's gut. As he grunted and the knife fell from her throat, she spun, and slammed a kick into his stomach.

He released her, crying out. She snatched the dagger from the ground and spun away. She threw herself at the group attacking Kace. She sliced open the arm of a Srinar, then spun and stabbed at a Thraxian.

She rolled up close to Kace. She loved her gladiator. She wasn't going to let them die here on this dirty floor.

She stood over him, holding the dagger up at the Thraxians. "Come on, you bastards."

"Rory…no."

She looked down at Kace. "Sorry, but we're in this together, pretty boy."

Chapter Fifteen

Pain. Kace couldn't separate the pains and aches anymore.

He knew he had broken ribs, and the blood loss was making him lightheaded, but he fought to stay conscious. His injuries were beyond his body's capabilities—he couldn't slow the blood flow or dampen the pain anymore.

All of it was blanked out by the panic he felt growing in his chest. He had to keep Rory safe. She was his heart, his everything, his reason for being.

And the two of them were going to die here.

He reached for her, pulling her closer. She lifted the puny dagger, fire in her eyes and a ferocious look on her face.

He knew she'd fight to the death.

Suddenly, the door to the room rattled. Everyone went still.

The imperator frowned. "Whoever it is, send them away." His burning gaze zeroed back in on Rory and Kace. "Time for you to die."

The door shuddered, like a great force had hit it. The Thraxians shifted nervously.

Suddenly, the door flew inward, mowing down the closest Thraxian.

Kace watched through his one good eye as Thorin charged into the room. He looked like a wild animal, his arms covered in dark scales.

The House of Galen gladiators rushed in behind him. Kace felt a sense of relief. Whatever happened now, Rory would be safe.

Raiden and Galen were in the lead. Lore and Nero followed. Saff strode in, a dark smile on her face as she wielded a sword, Harper by her side.

With a cry, the Thraxians and remaining Srinar charged forward.

"For honor and freedom," Raiden shouted.

"For honor and freedom," the other gladiators replied.

As the sound of fighting echoed around them, Kace felt Rory desperately trying to get her shoulder under his.

"Come on, pretty boy. On your feet."

"Really not pretty now."

She shot him a smile, but he saw the heartache behind it. She touched his beaten face. "You're always pretty to me."

"For the House of Thrax!" A Thraxian rushed at them.

Rory jumped to her feet and swung out with the dagger. She sliced the alien's arm open. He slapped a clawed hand over it, stumbling away.

With some grunting and groaning, Rory got her shoulder into Kace's side, and helped him to his feet. Pain was like flames licking at his body. He wasn't sure he could make it.

They moved out of the center of the mêlée,

shuffling slowly. He wasn't sure how far he could walk, but right now, for Rory, he kept putting one foot in front of the other.

As they neared the couch, he spotted Madeline. Whatever drugs she had been under the influence of had worn off, and she was blinking, trying to focus on her surroundings.

All of a sudden, the Thraxian imperator rushed in front of them.

He grabbed Madeline by the hair, and jerked her up on her feet. She screamed, showing the first sign of life. She started struggling.

"No," Rory cried.

The Thraxian pulled Madeline in front of him like a shield, edging toward the door that led away from the underground arena.

The coward was using her as a shield and a way out.

Kace had always known the Thraxians lacked honor, and this was a brilliant display of it.

"We have to stop them," Rory said.

"Rory…I can't fight."

She stared at his blood-soaked shirt. She had to know she was the only thing keeping him upright.

Suddenly, Lore appeared beside them. "Drak, military man. You aren't looking too good."

"Lore." A rush of dizziness washed over him. He had to ensure Rory's safety. "The House of Thrax were testing implants on their slaves and gladiators. Mind control implants called the Talos."

Lore cursed. "Don't worry about that now, we need to focus on getting you all fixed up." He reached for Kace.

"No," Kace said. "Rory's friend. The Imperator of the House of Thrax took her."

"Please, Lore," Rory implored him. "Catch him before he kills her. Bring her back."

Lore cursed, glancing to the doorway. "Okay, you two stay down until the others have cleared the room." He shoved a small field medical kit at Rory. "You need to stop the bleeding. By the looks of things, he can't afford to lose any more."

Rory took it. "I'll take care of him. You bring Madeline back."

Lore nodded, his tawny hair brushing his shoulders. "I will."

***

Lore

Lore moved stealthily through the doorway. It led into a long corridor.

Ahead, he heard a woman scream in pain.

Battle focus cooled his rage. On his world, women were to be worshipped, not hurt or abused.

He turned a corner, and saw the Thraxian imperator dragging a struggling woman beside him. She looked tiny compared to the giant alien.

Muttering a low curse, Lore pulled some powder from the pouches attached to his belt. He took three steps and tossed the powder into the air. It hung there for a second then it exploded, filling the corridor with a cloud of silver-gray smoke.

He heard the Thraxian cursing and shouting. He heard the woman coughing.

In the smoke, Lore saw shifting images—winged serpents, hunting cats, women with flowing hair and silver eyes. *May the totems of my people keep me safe.*

Keeping his eyes lowered, Lore rushed through the smoke. He slammed into the imperator. The alien let go of the woman and Lore tackled him to the ground.

As he pinned the larger man to the ground, Lore pulled his dagger from the sheath on his thigh.

"You chose the wrong women to hurt, and the wrong house to cross."

"Drak you, Galen scum."

With a cry, the woman surged forward and kicked the alien. "You bastard!"

Without any regret, Lore stabbed his dagger into the Thraxian's neck. Orange blood spurted. The imperator's eyes bulged and he coughed, blood staining his black lips.

He fell back, the noisy sound of his labored breaths escaping his ruined throat. It wouldn't kill him, but it would keep him down for the moment.

Lore turned to the woman.

She stood there, shaking, staring at him in the dissipating smoke. Her eyes were blank.

No. As he stared at her eyes—an interesting shade of blue that looked almost violet—he saw they weren't blank. They were filled with sadness and hurt.

"I'm here to help," he said.

She gave him a slow nod.

"You're Madeline. Harper, Regan, and Rory sent me."

He saw a faint shudder run through her body. She was short like the others, with a compact, feminine body. She tugged the minuscule dress around herself.

"It's time to get out of here. You with me?"

He saw her lift her chin, and spied a spark of life in her sad eyes. "What's your name?"

He heard the faintest snap of command in her voice, buried deep. Something told him his pretty survivor was used to giving orders. "Lore. My name is Lore."

"Lore." She said it like she was turning it over on her tongue.

"Actually, I have a very long family name that lists my mother, grandmother, and their mothers before them. Once we're safe, I'll tell you all about it." He held his hand out to her. "But only if you ask me nicely."

"I'm not nice," she whispered.

"*Dushla*, I don't believe that for a second."

With a shake of her head, she placed her hand in his. "I don't know what that word means."

He pulled her close, careful not to touch her. He could feel the tension in her body, her skittishness at being close to someone so big. She'd been held captive a long time, and he knew she was going to need time to heal. "It will be my pleasure to teach you the words of my people."

With his other hand, Lore snagged the

imperator's arm and dragged him behind them.

As they moved back toward the others, he could still hear fighting, although the sounds were less fierce than before.

Suddenly, Rory and Kace hobbled through the doorway.

Lore dumped the groaning Thraxian. "You two okay?"

"Fine." Rory barely blinked at the imperator, savage satisfaction on her face. Then her face softened and she held out a hand. "Madeline."

With a sob, Madeline threw herself at the other woman. Lore leaped forward to catch Kace, and Rory hugged the woman tightly.

"You're safe now," Rory murmured. "We're getting out of here. These are my friends."

Lore took a quick look at where Rory had patched Kace's wounds. The bandages were already soaked with blood.

"How bad?" he asked quietly.

"I'll survive," Kace answered. His gaze drifted to Rory. "I have a very good reason to live."

Lore smiled. Another gladiator succumbing to love. His sisters would love this. They all loved to see a strong man brought to his knees.

"Ready to get out of here?" Lore said, raising his voice.

"Hell yes." Rory moved back to Kace's side, her face concerned.

"Then let's head home," Lore said.

"Home," Madeline murmured. "Home." A broken sound.

Her pain stabbed at Lore. Helpless against it, Lore wrapped an arm around her. She was a tiny little thing, but he also sensed a steady strength in her. It had been beaten down, but he'd help her remember it.

Behind them, he heard the familiar clang of swords. Time to give his fellow gladiators a hand.

Lore pulled another illusion off his belt. He stepped closer to the door and tossed it inside.

This time, when the smoke exploded into the air, it caught fire, flames running along the flammable substance.

Cursing and shouting filled the air. A second later, the sounds of fighting stopped.

"Lore, how many times do I have to tell you not to use your illusions inside?" Galen muttered.

"You're welcome." Lore pulled Madeline through the door, watching as Rory helped Kace.

Galen appeared, flanked by Raiden and Saff. All of them were sporting a few wounds, but nothing major. He saw Madeline staring at them, her mouth dropping open.

He guessed they made for an intimidating sight—Galen with his scarred face and eye patch, Raiden with his tattoos, and Saff with her long braids. All three gladiators were holding blood-stained swords.

"Madeline." Harper rushed forward. "Are you okay?"

Madeline gripped Harper's arms, her bottom lip trembling. "It is so good to see you, Harper."

Harper squeezed the woman's hands. "You're

safe now."

Madeline nodded, and when she took a step closer, her knees went out from under her. Harper caught her before she fell, and Lore stepped forward and scooped her up.

She turned her head to face him. "I don't like being carried."

There was that faint sound of authority again. "Sorry, *dushla*." He held her tight against his chest. "Until you're back to full strength, I'm your own personal gladiator."

Violet eyes met his, held. Lore felt something spark there, a quiet whisper filled with promise.

Then her eyes widened, and moved over his shoulder.

He turned in time to see the Thraxian imperator stagger through the door, sword in hand. He bared his black teeth, his lips pulled tight over the tusks on either side of his mouth. He roared at them.

Galen stepped forward, and with a few swings of his sword, knocked the Thraxian back. Another thrust, and Galen's blade buried itself deep in the imperator's chest.

"Galen," Kace said, his voice wavering a little. "They were using an experimental mind control implant to control their gladiators. The Talos, they called it. It's why he wanted Rory and Madeline dead or gone. They have them, but they never worked."

Rory tapped her neck. "But the proof is still here, and he was worried someone would discover it."

"I will personally destroy your house." Galen said to the imperator, his tone the coldest and most lethal Lore had ever heard it. "One cardinal rule, and you can't even honor that. I will dismantle the House of Thrax, bit by bit. Every time more of you come, I will take you down. That is my vow."

He yanked his sword out, and the Thraxian slumped to the floor with a pained groan.

Galen shot the alien one last, hard glance. "You tell your people to stay away from mine, and that includes any women of Earth."

Lore tightened his hold on Madeline, felt her nails dig into his skin as she held on. He stared at his imperator for a moment, and then he grinned. "You are badass, G."

Galen raised a brow, then spun on his heels. "Let's get the hell out of here."

***

As they headed out into the crowd of the underground fight ring, the loud music assaulted Rory's ears. She pushed into Kace's side, doing her best to keep him on his feet.

A second later, Nero's big form appeared. He'd obviously been keeping watch on the main door to the winner's room. He lifted Kace's arm over his shoulders, and took the bulk of Kace's weight.

"How do we get out of here?" Kace yelled over the noise.

"We found a ramp that leads down here," Raiden answered. "A back entry used by the staff." He looked at Rory. "Your friend Hilea showed it to us."

"Hang on a second." Rory spun to face Galen. "There's another human from Earth here. A man. I saw him in the fight ring."

"What?" Harper shouldered forward. "Who?"

Rory swallowed. "Blaine Strong."

Harper rocked back on her feet, shock on her face. "No."

Rory knew Harper was friends with the man. She looked back at Galen. "He was on the security team with Harper at the space station. They're making him fight to the death in the ring. We can't leave him."

Galen looked torn, then nodded. They pushed through the crowd and reached the railing around the sunken pit.

Two large alien fighters were wrestling on the sand below, but neither one of them was Blaine. He was gone.

"No," Rory cried.

"We can't stay," Galen said. "Kace needs medical help, now. He has lost too much blood."

Harper gripped Rory's hand and squeezed it.

Rory looked at her friend. "Blaine was here, Harper. I saw him with my own eyes."

"I believe you." A spasm crossed Harper's face.

Galen cursed and grabbed a nearby spectator, jerking the thin man up on his toes. "There was a fighter here." Galen looked at Harper.

"He's tall with broad shoulders," Harper said. "Dark skin. Smooth like mine."

The man nodded his head, swallowing. "He won

three matches. They take them out to rest after three."

Rory released a breath. Blaine was still alive.

"Guy is a *machine* in the ring," the spectator added. "Crowd favorite. He's the champion of the fight ring."

Galen shoved the man away. "We have to go."

Harper's fingers tightened on Rory's. "We come back. We'll find him and rescue him, too."

Heart heavy, Rory moved back to Kace's side. They headed out and Galen led them to the back entrance they'd found down to the fight ring. They followed a spiral ramp upward. As they ascended, she felt dizziness trying to take over and gritted her teeth.

The ramp had doorways carved into the side of it, evenly spaced apart. Barely-covered men and women with dull, jaded eyes lolled in some of those openings. Other doors stood open, smoke wafting out of them and vacant-eyed people lounging inside.

Brothels and drug dens. Her gut cramped. There was a sense of hopelessness and despair that made her shiver.

She could have ended up here. Any one of the Fortuna abductees could have ended their nightmare here.

It made Rory realize how lucky she'd been to end up at the House of Galen.

And even more so, how incredibly lucky she'd been to find her friends and to find Kace. She looked up at him now. Even with his face swollen and in pain, he was still the most handsome, strong, and heroic man she'd ever met.

She was completely in love with her pretty-boy gladiator. She couldn't wait to get him healed and then show him exactly what he meant to her.

When they stepped out of the narrow tunnels and into the main part of the Kor Magna Markets, it was like a breath of fresh air.

Rory watched stall owners setting up for the day. Hell, they'd been underground all night. She sucked in the smells of cooking and felt nausea rise. She swallowed a few times, ready to be back aboveground.

She looked over at Madeline, tucked in Lore's strong arms. She looked broken and lost, nothing like the driven, haughty commander that they'd endured on Fortuna Station.

But they wouldn't let her stay broken. Everyone at the House of Galen would help Madeline, and help her find a way to heal.

They moved through the Kor Magna streets, streaks of gold lighting the dawn sky. Madeline blinked a bit now, her face lifted to the endless pale blue canopy. Rory kept a tight grip on Kace. He hadn't made a sound, but she knew he had to be in agony.

"Not too much farther," she told him.

His teeth were clenched as he nodded. "I can make it. I vowed to see you safe, and once you're back in the House of Galen, you will be."

"My hero," she whispered.

It wasn't long before they were back in the arena

tunnels, and the gray-and-red-cloaked guards were pushing open the double doors to the House of Galen. Their battered group stepped inside.

"Everything's going to be okay, pretty boy," Rory murmured to Kace. "The healers are going to get you fixed right up." She leaned in, pressing her lips close to his jaw, and lowering her voice. "And after that, it will be just you and me." She injected a sultry tone into her words. "I'm going to take good care of you."

His chest hitched. "Promise?"

"Oh, yes. I have a few new positions to show you."

His good eye gleamed.

"And I have something very important to tell you." Her belly jumped. She couldn't wait to tell him she was completely head over heels in love with him.

She sensed the others slowing down and she looked up. Ahead in the main entry area, she saw Regan's curvy form standing with a pair of House of Galen guards, and a small group of men.

The strangers were tall, with ramrod-straight postures. They all turned, and Rory swallowed a shocked gasp.

The resemblance to Kace was clear. They had similar features, with the same military bearings, and the same bronze skin.

Kace made a noise. "Chief Commander Daeron."

"Commander Tameron." The older Antarian's gaze ran over Kace's injured body, skating briefly over Rory without pausing. "It must have been a challenging battle."

"It was."

Rory felt like she'd swallowed a rock. These were Kace's people.

Regan stepped forward, wringing her hands. "Um, these men arrived while you were all out. They wanted to see Kace."

"Commanders? Why are you here?" Kace asked.

One of the other men stepped forward. "You'll be pleased to hear your training contract in the arena has been cut short, Commander Tameron. The battle with the Hemm'Darr has intensified, and we are recalling you to your position aboard our lead War Destroyer."

Rory saw conflicting emotions wash over Kace's face—duty, loyalty, regret. Now her stomach turned over in a sickening roll. She thought she was going to be sick.

"The Hemm'Darr are escalating their attacks," one of the other Antarians said. "Our people need our best soldiers."

Rory felt Kace's muscles tense beneath her hands. This was everything he lived for. His entire life had been about protecting his people.

She'd only been a brief blip in his life. An interesting diversion, one he'd fought not to succumb to.

Rory loved this man, and she wouldn't make this hard on him. She wouldn't let him betray his beliefs.

Her hero needed to be a hero.

She leaned up and pressed a chaste kiss to his

cheek. "Thank you for everything, Kace."

He turned to look at her, a strange, unreadable look on his face.

Steeling herself, she pulled away. "You are an amazing, noble man. I wish you the best of luck."

"Rory—"

Tears pricked at her eyes. *Dammit.* She *wouldn't* cry. "Promise me you'll stay safe." She felt her insides crumbling. "Be careful, pretty boy, and take care of yourself."

Before she broke down, Rory spun and ran back to her room.

All the way there, she tried to pretend that her heart wasn't shattered. She tried to tell herself she couldn't be bleeding inside over a man she'd only known for a few weeks.

But it didn't work. Back in her room, she raced into her bathroom and was violently sick. After she'd heaved up everything in her stomach, she rested her head against the cool tiles. Now the tears came.

She felt movement at her side and saw Hero appear, pressing against her. She grabbed him, holding him tight. As the sobs wracked her, Rory promised herself she would only cry this one time.

Then she'd pull herself back up and help her friends.

Chapter Sixteen

Rory stood with Regan and Harper in Medical, watching the Hermia healers treating Madeline.

The station commander sat huddled in a large chair, and refused to let go of Lore's hand. The gladiator sat beside her, talking to her in his smooth voice.

The healer stepped over to talk to them. "She's in shock." The healer's voice was low and fluid. "Physically, she's not in bad shape. She'll need some nutritional supplements for a while, but most of all, she'll just need some time."

"Thank you," Harper said.

"Fraser." Madeline's voice was a little shaky, but Rory thought it sounded more like the woman she'd known before.

Rory moved over to her.

Madeline lifted her gaze, tears brimming in her violet-blue eyes. "Thank you." She lifted her gaze. "Thanks to all of you for getting me out."

Rory touched the woman's arm. "You're safe here."

"Blaine. Blaine Strong was down there too."

Rory nodded, her throat tight. "We couldn't rescue him, but we will. We'll go back for him."

Madeline nodded. "How far are we from Earth? When can we go home?"

Aw, shit. Rory pulled in a deep breath and glanced at the others. Regan wrapped her arms around her middle, and a muscle ticked in Harper's jaw. They'd both had their turns informing someone else about their unfortunate reality.

Rory turned back to Madeline. "Too far. There's no way back to Earth. It would take roughly two hundred years."

"What?" Madeline's eyes went wide.

"I'm sorry—"

"That can't be! I have a son—" A sob tore from Madeline's throat.

Shit, Rory hadn't known Madeline had a child. "I really am sorry. The Thraxians used a transient wormhole to reach our solar system. It's since collapsed. There's no way back."

Madeline dissolved into ugly, heartbreaking sobs.

Lore dragged the woman into his lap and wrapped his arms around her. She buried her face against the gladiator's neck and held on tight.

"Go," he said, looking very at ease with the woman's tears. "I've got her."

Rory shuffled out with the others. Her heart cracked again as she absorbed Madeline's pain. Rory missed her family incredibly, but she didn't have a child. She couldn't conceive how bad that pain could possibly feel.

But with her heart already in pieces, this was more than Rory was able to cope with right now.

She turned to leave.

"Rory?" Harper's voice.

Rory stilled.

"I thought you'd want to know that Galen's sent people to find Hilea. He said she's welcome at the House of Galen."

Warmth fluttered in Rory's chest. "That's great. She probably won't come."

"He thought the same thing. He said he'd ensure she's taken care of."

"Great."

"And he's already making plans on how to rescue Blaine. We'll get him back."

Poor Blaine. "That's great." Rory turned to leave again. "I need some time alone. Kace is leaving and going back to his planet."

"No," Regan said. "I've watched the two of you together. He loves you, and you love him."

Rory imagined for a brief, brilliant second how it would feel for Kace to love her.

"He loves his planet," she said. "Even if he does feel something for me—" her voice broke "—I'm not going to make him choose." A wave of dizziness washed over her and made her stagger.

"Hey." Harper gripped her shoulder.

Rory shrugged her friend off. "I…just need some time alone." Before she fell apart for everyone to see. And Rory Fraser never fell apart.

She hurried along the corridor, her feet moving faster and faster. She thought about heading back to her room, or the gym, but everywhere and everything reminded her of Kace.

She slammed out of the doors of the House of Galen. The guards didn't stop her. She wasn't sure if it was the look on her face, or the fact that there was no longer a risk to her now.

Rory found herself running through the tunnels, and before she knew it, she stumbled out on top of the arena tower where Kace had taken her that other time she'd needed to escape and breathe.

The place where they'd first kissed.

She leaned against the stone railing, the wind hitting her face. She closed her eyes, breathing deep.

She refused to let the tears fall. They wouldn't help. Like Madeline, she just needed some time.

But deep down, Rory knew that the pieces of her heart would never fit back together the same way. Kace had worked his way in deep, and she didn't think she'd ever get him out. She pulled in a shaky breath. Hell, she didn't want to get him out.

She breathed in again, and this time, she imagined the smell of him. She choked back a sob.

Then, she sensed a presence behind her. Her eyes snapped open and she looked back.

And there he was.

Her hands clamped onto the stone. *Kace.*

***

Rory looked so beautiful, with the wind tugging at her red curls.

"You're all healed," she said.

He nodded. "The healers took care of me." He

still had a few faint aches in his ribs, but everything had mended nicely. His left eye was no longer swollen, his face clear of bruises.

"What are you doing here?" she demanded.

"You really think I'd just leave? Leave the House of Galen and Kor Magna in the blink of an eye?"

Her mouth opened, closed.

He took a step closer. "You really think I'd leave you like that?"

Her lips quivered. "You have your duty to your planet. I know it's everything you've ever worked for—"

"I'm falling in love with you, Rory."

She froze. "You don't believe in love. You said it doesn't exist."

"All my life, I've been told it doesn't exist. You've proven that very wrong. You've shown me what love means. What life means."

"Kace—"

He held his hands up. "I've lived for war. I was bred for it. Drak, I think you're right, they brainwash us to believe it."

She watched him steadily, and he saw tears glistening in her eyes.

"You've shown me that I can have more, Rory. I've seen the way you care, the way you live, the way you love. I *want* that."

He reached out and pulled her close. Her body was stiff, her heart hammering against his chest.

"I want to live, Rory." He couldn't stop himself from kissing her, pulling her taste inside him. "I love you."

Her hands gripped his chest. "Oh, God, Kace, I love you, too."

"Thank the Creators," he murmured against her lips.

Suddenly, they were tearing at each other's clothes. "Yes." Her voice was husky, as she yanked open his trousers.

Kace took seconds to strip her trousers off and one more second to tear her underwear to shreds. She gasped, jerking against him.

His pretty, sexy woman liked that.

He backed her against the wall and lifted her. She wrapped her legs around his hips, his cock pushing against her hot center.

She moaned, moving against him.

"So greedy."

"For you, I always am."

Kace needed her. He needed to feel her around him, hot and alive and vital.

He plunged inside her.

Rory let out a choked cry, her hands digging into his shoulders. There was no time for gentleness or finesse. Kace needed to claim his woman, and ensure she knew exactly who she belonged to.

He thrust inside her, glorying at her cries and the tight clasp of her body.

He felt his release charging home, his vision dimming. "Rory."

"I'm here, Kace."

He reached between their bodies, and as soon as he touched her swollen clit, she screamed his name, her body clamping down on his.

Kace leaned forward, burying his face in her neck, and as his release hit, his hips lunged forward, and he poured himself inside her.

Rory Fraser was his. And he'd do whatever he had to do to ensure everyone knew that.

Especially Rory herself.

***

When Kace moved, pulling her into his arms, she felt flushed and happy. She leaned into his strength, listening to the rapid beat of his heart beneath her ear.

"I've corrupted you," she said. "Here you are, the sensible military soldier having a quickie."

"A quickie?" he asked with a frown.

"It's an Earth term for…never mind." Familiar dread filled her. "Kace, was this goodbye?"

"What?" He lifted his head and set her on her feet. He cupped her cheeks. "No. This was me telling you I'm staying. With you. Forever."

God. She could barely breathe. "They'll let you do that? The military will just let you go that easily?"

"No."

For a moment, his face looked so remote, so blank.

"Tell me?" she whispered.

"I informed my superiors that I am leaving the Antarian military and staying here on Carthago."

Her mouth dropped open. *He what?*

He swallowed. "Needless to say, they banished

me from my planet. I am no longer welcome on Antar."

She gasped. "Oh, my God. Kace, are you sure this is what you want?" He was giving up his *planet* for her?

He smiled. "Yes."

"You're sure you want to stay here with me?" Her hands tightened on him. "Be sure, pretty boy, because if you stay, I'm never going to let you go."

He cupped her jaw, pulling her face up to his, lips brushing hers. "You are mine, Rory Fraser. Now and always. I know you have lots more living to show me."

She winked. "And lots more positions."

He smiled back. "I love you so much it hurts."

God, he was perfect. Suddenly, a wave of dizziness washed over her, almost driving her to her knees.

He muttered a curse and pulled her into his arms. "Rory? What's wrong?"

"Dizzy."

"Are you hurt?"

She shook her head. "No. But it's been a hell of a day. I'm sure I just need some rest." She'd never felt this drained before.

"No, you'll see a healer first." He helped her back into her clothes before sorting out his own. Then he hitched his arm under her knees, and headed for the stairs.

Rory argued with him, tried to cajole him into bed, but her stubborn, overprotective gladiator wasn't having it any other way.

When he carried her into the Medical center, her friends were still there with Madeline.

Rory rolled her eyes at them all.

They were all grinning at her and Kace. Even Madeline managed a smile. Lore was still sprawled in a chair as well, and he looked highly amused.

Kace set Rory down on one of the benches on the other side of the room. "She had a dizzy spell."

Suddenly, a small body shot through the door and leaped onto the bed beside Rory. The Hermia healer looked shocked.

Rory patted Hero's head. "This is my pet. He can sort of tell when I'm hurt or upset." She smiled at Kace. "I'm lucky to have two personal heroes of my own."

The Hermia healer straightened and moved closer with a quiet rustle of robes, holding a handheld scanner. After waving it over Rory, the healer frowned. "You had your medical checkup when you arrived at the House of Galen?"

"Yes." Rory frowned. What the hell was wrong with her?

"You had the contraceptive implant put in?"

"Yes."

The healer studied the scanner screen. "I need to get you some vitamin supplements. You are going to need to bulk up on your vitamins to carry the child."

Rory went still, and saw Kace do the same.

"Carry the…?" Rory said incredulously.

The healer gave a calm nod. "You're pregnant. The child appears to be half Antarian. They grow at a fast rate, so even though the pregnancy appears very new, it is already detectable."

Rory cocked her head. She must not have heard correctly. "I'm what?"

The healer's face was calm and composed. "With child."

Rory reached over and slapped Kace's chest. "You got me pregnant!"

Her gladiator was staring at her, speechless, shock stamped over his handsome features.

Rory looked back at the healer. "But I had the implant to prevent this."

The healer nodded. "Antarians have very persistent reproductive cells. They are reported to be able to circumvent most standard contraceptives. On their world, the Antarian military regulate their procreation. Since Kace has never indulged in intercourse here on Carthago, it has never been a problem."

Rory narrowed her gaze on Kace. "Did you know you had super-soldier sperm?"

He still looked shocked.

She dropped her face into her hands. "Abducted by aliens, sold into slavery, rescued, people trying to kill me, and now I'm pregnant with an alien baby."

She felt Kace's big hand brush over her hair. "Rory, I'm sorry."

She lifted her head and smiled. "I'm not." She was going to have a baby. Kace's baby. *Their* baby.

"You're not?" He looked confused.

Her poor gladiator. Rory had always been one to

roll with life's punches. And at least this blow was a welcome one, no matter how much of a surprise it was.

She pulled his big hand down to her belly. "A baby, Kace. We made a baby."

Wonder drifted over his features. He leaned down and kissed her. "Every moment of every day, you teach me more about how to live. I love you."

"I love you, too."

"What is going on?" Harper demanded, striding across to them. Regan followed behind her, looking concerned.

"Kace knocked me up," Rory told them.

Her friend and cousin both blinked, mouths dropping open.

"You're going to have a *baby*!" Regan's voice rose to an excited scream.

"Yep."

Her friends hugged her and a dazed Kace, and Regan started babbling on about babies and possible differences in alien pregnancies.

The doors to Medical slammed open and Galen, Raiden, Thorin, and Saff strode in.

"What in drak's name is going on in here?" Galen demanded. "The healers told me to get down here immediately."

Saff took in Kace's hand spread over Rory's belly before jerking her gaze up to her fight partner's face. "By the Creators, Kace impregnated his Earth girl."

The other gladiators all froze.

Kace grinned. "We're having a baby."

As more talking broke out around them, Rory leaned into Kace. He pressed his lips to hers. "Rory, I know nothing about being a father."

"Don't worry, Kace. We'll work all this out together. One day at a time."

He nodded. "I am a fast learner."

"All you have to do is love our child, and me. The rest will fall into place."

"I do love you. Don't stop loving me."

"Never," she told him. "I have lots more living to show you yet."

A sexy smile transformed his face. "I look forward to that."

"It probably won't be tidy and orderly—" At that moment, Hero butted his head against them, trying to worm closer.

Kace's hands tightened on her. "Good."

She kissed him again. "Hang on, pretty boy. I think our ride is going to be a wild one."

I hope you enjoyed Kace and Rory's story!

Galactic Gladiators continues with PROTECTOR, starring showman gladiator Lore, and will be out in early 2017.

For more action-packed romance, read on for a preview of the first chapter of *Marcus*, the first book in my bestselling Hell Squad series.

Don't miss out! For updates about new releases, action romance info, free books, and other fun stuff, sign up for my VIP mailing list and get your *free box set* containing three action-packed romances.

Visit here to get started:
www.annahackettbooks.com

FREE BOX SET DOWNLOAD

JOIN THE ACTION-PACKED ADVENTURE!

Formats: Kindle, ePub, PDF

Preview – Hell Squad: Marcus

READY FOR ANOTHER?

IN THE AFTERMATH OF AN ALIEN INVASION:

HEROES WILL RISE... WHEN THEY HAVE SOMEONE TO LIVE FOR

Her team was under attack.

Elle Milton pressed her fingers to her small earpiece. "Squad Six, you have seven more raptors inbound from the east." Her other hand gripped the edge of her comp screen, showing the enhanced drone feed.

She watched, her belly tight, as seven glowing red dots converged on the blue ones huddled together in the burned-out ruin of an office building in downtown Sydney. Each blue dot was a squad member and one of them was their leader.

"Marcus? Do you copy?" Elle fought to keep her voice calm. No way she'd let them hear her alarm.

"Roger that, Elle." Marcus' gravelly voice filled her ear. Along with the roar of laser fire. "We see them."

She sagged back in her chair. This was the worst part. Just sitting there knowing that Marcus and the others were fighting for their lives. In the six months she'd been comms officer for the squad, she'd worked hard to learn the ropes. But there were days she wished she was out there, aiming a gun and taking out as many alien raptors as she could.

You're not a soldier, Ellianna. No, she was a useless party-girl-turned-survivor. She watched as a red dot disappeared off the screen, then another, and another. She finally drew a breath. Marcus and his team were the experienced soldiers. She'd just be a big fat liability in the field.

But she was a damn good comms officer.

Just then, a new cluster of red dots appeared near the team. She tapped the screen, took a measurement. "Marcus! More raptors are en route. They're about one kilometer away. North." God, would these invading aliens ever leave them alone?

"Shit," Marcus bit out. Then he went silent.

She didn't know if he was thinking or fighting. She pictured his rugged, scarred face creased in thought as he formulated a plan.

Then his deep, rasping voice was back. "Elle, we need an escape route and an evac now. Shaw's been hit in the leg, Cruz is carrying him. We can't engage more raptors."

She tapped the screen rapidly, pulling up drone images and archived maps. *Escape route, escape route*. Her mind clicked through the options. She knew Shaw was taller and heavier than Cruz, but the armor they wore had slim-line exoskeletons built into them allowing the soldiers to lift heavier loads and run faster and longer than normal. She tapped the screen again. *Come on*. She needed somewhere safe for a Hawk quadcopter to set down and pick them up.

"Elle? We need it now!"

Just then her comp beeped. She looked at the image and saw a hazy patch of red appear in the broken shell of a nearby building. The heat sensor had detected something else down there. Something big.

Right next to the team.

She touched her ear. "Rex! Marcus, a rex has just woken up in the building beside you."

"Fuck! Get us out of here. Now."

Oh, God. Elle swallowed back bile. Images of rexes, with their huge, dinosaur-like bodies and mouths full of teeth, flashed in her head.

More laser fire ripped through her earpiece and she heard the wild roar of the awakening beast.

Block it out. She focused on the screen. Marcus needed her. The team needed her.

"Run past the rex." One hand curled into a tight fist, her nails cutting into her skin. "Go through its hiding place."

"Through its nest?" Marcus' voice was incredulous. "You know how territorial they are."

"It's the best way out. On the other side you'll find a railway tunnel. Head south along it about eight hundred meters, and you'll find an emergency exit ladder that you can take to the surface. I'll have a Hawk pick you up there."

A harsh expulsion of breath. "Okay, Elle. You've gotten us out of too many tight spots for me to doubt you now."

His words had heat creeping into her cheeks. His praise…it left her giddy. In her life BAI—before alien invasion—no one had valued her opinions. Her father, her mother, even her almost-fiancé, they'd all thought her nothing more than a pretty ornament. Hell, she *had* been a silly, pretty party girl.

And because she'd been inept, her parents were dead. Elle swallowed. A year had passed since that horrible night during the first wave of the alien attack, when their giant ships had appeared in the skies. Her parents had died that night, along with most of the world.

"Hell Squad, ready to go to hell?" Marcus called out.

"Hell, yeah!" the team responded. "The devil needs an ass-kicking!"

"Woo-hoo!" Another voice blasted through her headset, pulling her from the past. "Ellie, baby, this dirty alien's nest stinks like Cruz's socks. You should be here."

A smile tugged at Elle's lips. Shaw Baird always

knew how to ease the tension of a life-or-death situation.

"Oh, yeah, Hell Squad gets the best missions," Shaw added.

Elle watched the screen, her smile slipping. Everyone called Squad Six the Hell Squad. She was never quite sure if it was because they were hellions, or because they got sent into hell to do the toughest, dirtiest missions.

There was no doubt they were a bunch of rebels. Marcus had a rep for not following orders. Just the previous week, he'd led the squad in to destroy a raptor outpost but had detoured to rescue survivors huddled in an abandoned hospital that was under attack. At the debrief, the general's yelling had echoed through the entire base. Marcus, as always, had been silent.

"Shut up, Shaw, you moron." The deep female voice carried an edge.

Elle had decided there were two words that best described the only female soldier on Hell Squad—loner and tough. Claudia Frost was everything Elle wasn't. Elle cleared her throat. "Just get yourselves back to base."

As she listened to the team fight their way through the rex nest, she tapped in the command for one of the Hawk quadcopters to pick them up.

The line crackled. "Okay, Elle, we're through. Heading to the evac point."

Marcus' deep voice flowed over her and the tense muscles in her shoulders relaxed a fraction. They'd be back soon. They were okay. He was okay.

She pressed a finger to the blue dot leading the team. "The bird's en route, Marcus."

"Thanks. See you soon."

She watched on the screen as the large, black shadow of the Hawk hovered above the ground and the team boarded. The rex was headed in their direction, but they were already in the air.

Elle stood and ran her hands down her trousers. She shot a wry smile at the camouflage fabric. It felt like a dream to think that she'd ever owned a very expensive, designer wardrobe. And heels—God, how long had it been since she'd worn heels? These days, fatigues were all that hung in her closet. Well-worn ones, at that.

As she headed through the tunnels of the underground base toward the landing pads, she forced herself not to run. She'd see him—them—soon enough. She rounded a corner and almost collided with someone.

"General. Sorry, I wasn't watching where I was going."

"No problem, Elle." General Adam Holmes had a military-straight bearing he'd developed in the United Coalition Army and a head of dark hair with a brush of distinguished gray at his temples. He was classically handsome, and his eyes were a piercing blue. He was the top man in this last little outpost of humanity. "Squad Six on their way back?"

"Yes, sir." They fell into step.

"And they secured the map?"

God, Elle had almost forgotten about the map.

"Ah, yes. They got images of it just before they came under attack by raptors."

"Well, let's go welcome them home. That map might just be the key to the fate of mankind."

They stepped into the landing areas. Staff in various military uniforms and civilian clothes raced around. After the raptors had attacked, bringing all manner of vicious creatures with them to take over the Earth, what was left of mankind had banded together.

Whoever had survived now lived here in an underground base in the Blue Mountains, just west of Sydney, or in the other, similar outposts scattered across the planet. All arms of the United Coalition's military had been decimated. In the early days, many of the surviving soldiers had fought amongst themselves, trying to work out who outranked whom. But it didn't take long before General Holmes had unified everyone against the aliens. Most squads were a mix of ranks and experience, but the teams eventually worked themselves out. Most didn't even bother with titles and rank anymore.

Sirens blared, followed by the clang of metal. Huge doors overhead retracted into the roof.

A Hawk filled the opening, with its sleek gray body and four spinning rotors. It was near-silent, running on a small thermonuclear engine. It turned slowly as it descended to the landing pad.

Her team was home.

She threaded her hands together, her heart beating a little faster.

Marcus was home.

***

Marcus Steele wanted a shower and a beer.

Hot, sweaty and covered in raptor blood, he leaped down from the Hawk and waved at his team to follow. He kept a sharp eye on the medical team who raced out to tend to Shaw. Dr. Emerson Green was leading them, her white lab coat snapping around her curvy body. The blonde doctor caught his gaze and tossed him a salute.

Shaw was cursing and waving them off, but one look from Marcus and the lanky Australian sniper shut his mouth.

Marcus swung his laser carbine over his shoulder and scraped a hand down his face. Man, he'd kill for a hot shower. Of course, he'd have to settle for a cold one since they only allowed hot water for two hours in the morning in order to conserve energy. But maybe after that beer he'd feel human again.

"Well done, Squad Six." Holmes stepped forward. "Steele, I hear you got images of the map."

Holmes might piss Marcus off sometimes, but at least the guy always got straight to the point. He was a general to the bone and always looked spit and polish. Everything about him screamed money and a fancy education, so not surprisingly, he tended to rub the troops the wrong way.

Marcus pulled the small, clear comp chip from his pocket. "We got it."

Then he spotted her.

Shit. It was always a small kick in his chest. His gaze traveled up Elle Milton's slim figure, coming to rest on a face he could stare at all day. She wasn't very tall, but that didn't matter. Something about her high cheekbones, pale-blue eyes, full lips, and rain of chocolate-brown hair…it all worked for him. Perfectly. She was beautiful, kind, and far too good to be stuck in this crappy underground maze of tunnels, dressed in hand-me-down fatigues.

She raised a slim hand. Marcus shot her a small nod.

"Hey, Ellie-girl. Gonna give me a kiss?"

Shaw passed on an iono-stretcher hovering off the ground and Marcus gritted his teeth. The tall, blond sniper with his lazy charm and Aussie drawl was popular with the ladies. Shaw flashed his killer smile at Elle.

She smiled back, her blue eyes twinkling and Marcus' gut cramped.

Then she put one hand on her hip and gave the sniper a head-to-toe look. She shook her head. "I think you get enough kisses."

Marcus released the breath he didn't realize he was holding.

"See you later, Sarge." Zeke Jackson slapped Marcus on the back and strolled past. His usually-silent twin, Gabe, was beside him. The twins, both former Coalition Army Special Forces soldiers, were deadly in the field. Marcus was damned happy to have them on his squad.

"Howdy, Princess." Claudia shot Elle a smirk as

she passed.

Elle rolled her eyes. "Claudia."

Cruz, Marcus' second-in-command and best friend from their days as Coalition Marines, stepped up beside Marcus and crossed his arms over his chest. He'd already pulled some of his lightweight body armor off, and the ink on his arms was on display.

The general nodded at Cruz before looking back at Marcus. "We need Shaw back up and running ASAP. If the raptor prisoner we interrogated is correct, that map shows one of the main raptor communications hubs." There was a blaze of excitement in the usually-stoic general's voice. "It links all their operations together."

Yeah, Marcus knew it was big. Destroy the hub, send the raptor operations into disarray.

The general continued. "As soon as the tech team can break the encryption on the chip and give us a location for the raptor comms hub—" his piercing gaze leveled on Marcus "—I want your team back out there to plant the bomb."

Marcus nodded. He knew if they destroyed the raptors' communications it gave humanity a fighting chance. A chance they desperately needed.

He traded a look with Cruz. Looked like they were going out to wade through raptor gore again sooner than anticipated.

Man, he really wanted that beer.

Then Marcus' gaze landed on Elle again. He didn't keep going out there for himself, or Holmes. He went so people like Elle and the other civilian survivors had a chance. A chance to do more than simply survive.

"Shaw's wound is minor. Doc Emerson should have him good as new in an hour or so." Since the advent of the nano-meds, simple wounds could be healed in hours, rather than days and weeks. They carried a dose of the microscopic medical machines on every mission, but only for dire emergencies. The nano-meds had to be administered and monitored by professionals or they were just as likely to kill you from the inside than heal you.

General Holmes nodded. "Good."

Elle cleared her throat. "There's no telling how long it will take to break the encryption. I've been working with the tech team and even if they break it, we may not be able to translate it all. We're getting better at learning the raptor language but there are still huge amounts of it we don't yet understand."

Marcus' jaw tightened. There was always something. He knew Noah Kim—their resident genius computer specialist—and his geeks were good, but if they couldn't read the damn raptor language...

Holmes turned. "Steele, let your team have some downtime and be ready the minute Noah has anything."

"Yes, sir." As the general left, Marcus turned to Cruz. "Go get yourself a beer, Ramos."

"Don't need to tell me more than once, *amigo.* I would kill for some of my dad's tamales to go with it." Something sad flashed across a face all the women in the base mooned over, then he grimaced and a bone-deep weariness colored his words. "Need to wash the raptor off me, first." He tossed Marcus a casual salute, Elle a smile, and strode out.

Marcus frowned after his friend and absently started loosening his body armor.

Elle moved up beside him. "I can take the comp chip to Noah."

"Sure." He handed it to her. When her fingers brushed his he felt the warmth all the way through him. Hell, he had it bad. Thankfully, he still had his armor on or she'd see his cock tenting his pants.

"I'll come find you as soon as we have something." She glanced up at him. Smiled. "Are you going to rec night tonight? I hear Cruz might even play guitar for us."

The Friday-night gathering was a chance for everyone to blow off a bit of steam and drink too much homebrewed beer. And Cruz had an unreal talent with a guitar, although lately Marcus hadn't seen the man play too much.

Marcus usually made an appearance at these parties, then left early to head back to his room to study raptor movements or plan the squad's next missions. "Yeah, I'll be there."

"Great." She smiled. "I'll see you there, then." She hurried out clutching the chip.

He stared at the tunnel where she'd exited for a long while after she disappeared, and finally ripped his chest armor off. Ah, on second thought, maybe going to the rec night wasn't a great idea. Watching her pretty face and captivating smile would drive him crazy. He cursed under his breath. He really needed that cold shower.

As he left the landing pads, he reminded himself he should be thinking of the mission. Destroy the hub and kill more aliens. Rinse and repeat. Death and killing, that was about all he knew.

He breathed in and caught a faint trace of Elle's floral scent. She was clean and fresh and good. She always worried about them, always had a smile, and she was damned good at providing their comms and intel.

She was why he fought through the muck every day. So she could live and the goodness in her would survive. She deserved more than blood and death and killing.

And she sure as hell deserved more than a battled-scarred, bloodstained soldier.

Hell Squad

Marcus

Cruz

Gabe

Reed

Roth

Noah

Shaw

Holmes

Niko

Finn

Devlin

Also by Anna Hackett

Treasure Hunter Security

Undiscovered

Uncharted

Unexplored

Unfathomed

Galactic Gladiators

Gladiator

Warrior

Hero

Protector

Hell Squad

Marcus

Cruz

Gabe

Reed

Roth

Noah

Shaw

Holmes

Niko

Finn

Devlin

The Anomaly Series

Time Thief

Mind Raider

Soul Stealer

Salvation

Anomaly Series Box Set

The Phoenix Adventures

Among Galactic Ruins

At Star's End

In the Devil's Nebula

On a Rogue Planet

Beneath a Trojan Moon

Beyond Galaxy's Edge

On a Cyborg Planet

Return to Dark Earth

On a Barbarian World

Lost in Barbarian Space

Through Uncharted Space

Perma Series

Winter Fusion

The WindKeepers Series

Wind Kissed, Fire Bound

Taken by the South Wind

Tempting the West Wind

Defying the North Wind

Claiming the East Wind

Standalone Titles
Savage Dragon
Hunter's Surrender
One Night with the Wolf

Anthologies
A Galactic Holiday
Moonlight (UK only)
Vampire Hunter (UK only)
Awakening the Dragon (UK Only)

For more information visit AnnaHackettBooks.com

About the Author

I'm a USA Today bestselling author and I'm passionate about ***action romance***. I love stories that combine the thrill of falling in love with the excitement of action, danger and adventure. I'm a sucker for that moment when the team is walking in slow motion, shoulder-to-shoulder heading off into battle.

I write about people overcoming unbeatable odds and achieving seemingly impossible goals. I like to believe it's possible for all of us to do the same.

My books are mixture of action, adventure and sexy romance and they're recommended for anyone who enjoys fast-paced stories where the boy wins the girl at the end (or sometimes the girl wins the boy!)

For release dates, action romance info, free books, and other fun stuff, sign up for the latest news here:

Website: AnnaHackettBooks.com

Lightning Source UK Ltd.
Milton Keynes UK
UKHW041815170219
337497UK00001B/8/P